The Sky Is Falling

Books by Barbara Corcoran

The Sky Is Falling

BARBARA CORCORAN

A JEAN KARL BOOK
Atheneum   1988   New York

Atheneum
Macmillan Publishing Company
866 Third Avenue, New York, NY 10022
Collier Macmillan Canada, Inc.
First Edition
Printed in the United States of America
10 9 8 7 6 5 4 3 2 1

Design and calligraphy by Ismar David, ABCD Studio

Library of Congress Cataloging-in-Publication Data
Corcoran, Barbara.
    The sky is falling/Barbara Corcoran.—1st ed. p.   cm.
    Summary: In Boston during the early days of the Great Depression,
Annah's affluent life-style comes to an abrupt end when her father
loses his banking job. Annah is sent to live with her aunt on a
New Hampshire island, where she meets a destitute but spunky girl
named Dodie.
    "A Jean Karl book."
    ISBN 0–689–31388–8 [1. Depression—1929—Fiction.
2. Friendship—Fiction. 3. New England—Fiction.] I. Title.
PZ7.C814Skn 1988 [Fic]—dc19   87–33358 CIP   AC

To my hometown

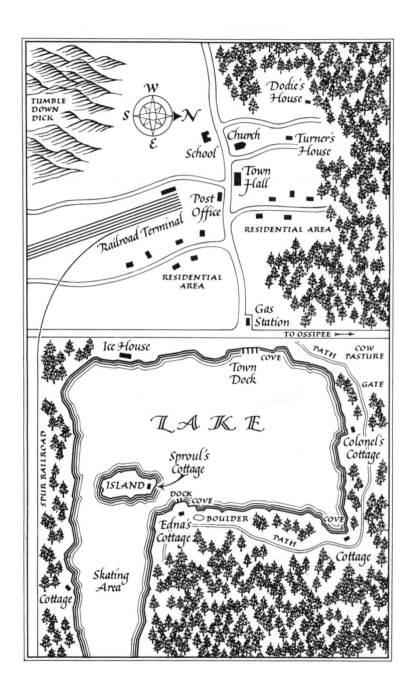

The Sky Is Falling

ANNAH circled the date in her diary and printed carefully on the top line: ANNAH PERRY, FOURTEEN YEARS OLD ON THIS DAY, 1931. The grandfather clock on the stairs chimed four. She heard a car drive into the yard, but she still lingered, touching the magical date with her finger. Earlier in the afternoon her brother Herb had said, "They're making history on your birthday, Sis." He had been listening to the radio. "Thomas Edison is dead. Seventy-five thousand Nazi stormtroopers are rampaging in Germany, and Columbia is beating the stuffing out of Dartmouth." He did not add, because he did not know, that a few minutes before their uncle Herbert had jumped out of his twenty-second-story office in Boston's financial district.

Annah wished Mr. Edison had picked a different day to die. She had no idea who or what the Nazis were. But she did feel sorry about the football game. Herb was a freshman at Dartmouth, and he was looking glum.

Still, a little later when the guests had arrived for her birthday party, she thought it was one of the nicest days of her life. Her parents had given her a shiny blue bicycle with a carrier basket on the front, and a leather-bound copy of her favorite book, *Wuthering Heights*. And here were all her favorite friends sitting around her while she opened her presents. And her handsome brother, whom all her friends had a crush on, was home

3

for the first time since he'd started college, sprawled in the big leather chair in his white sweater with the big D. She hadn't realized until he came in the door last night how much she had missed him.

She reached for the package her best friend, Tillie, had brought. Tillie giggled and sat on the edge of her chair.

"It's heavy," Annah said.

Richie, who had been her friend since they were babies, said, "It's a slab of cement."

"It isn't really, is it?" Betsy asked. Both Richie and Tillie groaned. Leave it to Betsy to make the dumb remark.

Annah unwrapped the gift paper and folded it neatly.

"Hurry up," Peter said. "The suspense is killing me."

She smiled. Peter was new in town, and this was the first time he had been in her house. She'd been glad when he looked around approvingly and said, "Nifty house." Some people thought their 1880s house, with its odd-shaped rooms, the winding staircase, and the turrets, was peculiar, but she loved it. She wished she could show him her round bedroom in one of the turrets, but taking a strange boy—or any boy except Richie—into her bedroom for even the most innocent purpose would give her mother a conniption fit.

She peeked into the gift box and said, "Bookends! Til! Just what I need." She took them out. They were heavy grayish green metal, shaped like ships. "Oh, I love them." She leaned over and gave Tillie a hug.

"Does anybody ever say," Richie asked, " 'Of all the things I never wanted, this is it'?"

4

"But I do want them," Annah said, as the others laughed. "My room has piles of books sitting on the floor, and they're always falling over." She held them up. "Look, Herb."

"I see. They're very handsome." Herb was standing now with one elbow on the wide mahogany mantel over the big fireplace, looking at them benevolently, like a grown-up, Annah thought. He's grown up in only a couple of months.

At that moment, the telephone rang in their father's den across the hall. A few minutes later, as Annah was exclaiming over the salmon-colored cashmere cardigan that Richie had picked out for her, her mother came into the room looking pale. Annah pulled her blonde hair back behind her ears and held up the sweater. "Look, Mother, isn't it beautiful?"

"Lovely," her mother said in a strained voice.

"What's the matter?" Annah said. "What's happened?"

Herb was already moving forward.

"Herbert, your father wants you," his mother said.

Herb followed her quickly out of the room.

"What's up?" Richie said.

Annah shrugged. "Oh, you know how grown-ups are. Every problem is a crisis." But she felt a bit nervous. Her mother was indeed inclined to make mountains out of molehills, but she had looked strange. To restore the mood of the party, she said, "Hey, Rich, I'm a year older than you again."

Their birthdays were only five weeks apart, and when they were little, she always made him admit she was a year older for that brief time. He never let her forget the year she had got him flat on his back on the ground and tickled him till he shrieked, "All right! You're six, I'm five." But now he was six inches taller than she was and about twice as broad in the shoulders.

Annah opened Peter's present: blue wool knee socks with the little arrows up the ankles that were called clocks, although Annah didn't know why they were called such a dumb name. "They are perfect, Peter. Just what I need."

"Just exactly what I wanted," Richie echoed. They all laughed.

"They don't match the sweater," Richie said. Richie wanted to be a stage designer, and he cared about things like colors going together.

"Take back the sweater," Peter said.

Margaret came in from the kitchen, wearing her frilly apron and a broad smile. "Eats in the dining room," she said.

She had fixed up the table with crepe paper streamers and place cards and tiny paper baskets of jelly beans, the way she always did. Margaret had been with them since Annah was five, and Annah loved her more than anybody in the world except her own family. Margaret almost *was* her own family.

"It's beautiful, Margaret," she said. Margaret, who was even smaller than Annah, beamed. Annah gave her a hug. "Remember my fifth birthday?" she said.

Margaret laughed. "I do indeed. Me only two weeks over from Ireland, and never having ice cream before in me whole life." She brought in the birthday cake, fourteen candles and one to grow on, while the others sang, "Happy birthday."

"Well, we aren't going to wait for Herbert," Annah

said when Margaret brought in the baked Alaska. But she was a little worried. It wasn't like Herb to miss the ice cream and cake.

Later, when Peter's mother came to take everybody home in their new Buick touring car, neither Herb nor Annah's mother had put in an appearance. Annah was embarrassed at what she was afraid looked like rudeness. They didn't know Peter's parents well; they were Congregationalists and lived on the other side of town beyond the Hunt Club. It was not like Annah's mother not to be a proper hostess.

She tried to make up for it by being extra polite and thanking everybody again. Soon they were gone, and she went to find her family.

They were still in the den, and her father was on the telephone. Her mother had been crying.

"What is it?" Annah said.

Herb took her by the arm and walked her out to the kitchen, where Margaret was washing up the dishes from the party.

Margaret looked over her shoulder at them. "He could have picked a better day than your birthday," she said.

"Who?" Annah said.

"Your uncle Herbert."

Herb sat down at the kitchen table and ran his finger around the inside of the frosting bowl. "Uncle Herbert killed himself."

Annah was stunned. It was not that she felt close to Uncle Herbert. She had never thought he really liked children, although when he came to visit he always brought them a box of gumdrops and said how they'd grown, the right things according to the grown-up code. And he sent them checks at Christmas, a fairly big one for Herb, who was named for him. "Did he shoot himself or what?"

"Jumped out of his office window. The twenty-second floor."

She felt sick. Uncle Herbert was always a dapper man, Brooks Brothers suits and Sulka ties, slicked-down blond hair and a tiny Ronald Colman mustache. She could hardly bear to think of him spattered all over the cobblestones. "What was he doing in his office on a weekend?"

Herb shrugged. "Getting ready to jump, I guess."

"Well, you have to give him that," Margaret said. "On a weekday he'd have crashed into people and likely hurt them."

"Why would he do a thing like that?" Annah said.

"Last Monday England suspended gold payments."

She waited, but he didn't go on. "And?"

"He was a broker. It's a big deal in international financial markets. A lot of brokers are jumping out windows and blowing their brains out these days."

Herb was trying to sound as if he were not upset, but he looked pale and there were lines around his mouth that came when he was trying not to show his feelings.

"You're the namesake," Margaret said. She took the frosting bowl away from him and put it into the soapy water in the sink.

Annah noticed how pretty she looked, and wondered if she had been seeing Johnny LeFaver again. She had been engaged to him once, but she broke it off when he wouldn't lay off the moonshine booze.

8

"So you'll get a bundle, I shouldn't wonder," Margaret said.

"If he had a bundle, he wouldn't have jumped," Herb said.

Margaret sighed. "There is that. The world is upside down, indeed."

"Eight million people without jobs." Herb frowned at Annah.

"It's not my fault." She felt uneasy, as if she had done something wrong without even knowing it. Maybe been too happy? "Richie and his mother were on Boston Common the other day, and a man asked them for a dime. All Rich's mother had was a twenty-dollar bill and seven cents, so she gave him the seven cents." Now that she'd said it, she didn't know why she had repeated that story. Richie thought it was funny because his mother didn't see anything wrong with it, but it had bothered Annah even at the time. "The guy seemed glad to get it," Richie had said. Glad to get seven cents? Nowadays hoboes stopped at the back door much more often than they used to. Whoever was in the kitchen, Annah or Margaret or Annah's mother, always asked them in for something to eat. Her father said the hoboes marked the houses some way; the ones that were "easy marks" got the most hoboes. But they worried her. A lot of them weren't like the old ones who roamed the country from choice; a lot of these men had lost their jobs, and they were really hungry.

Sternly, Herb said, "Richie's dad could lose his cushy job tomorrow and end up on the Common selling apples."

"That's silly," Annah said. "He's got a good job."

"So did Uncle Herbert."

"Leave the child alone," Margaret said. "It's her birthday." She picked up one of the favors that hadn't been used, the kind you blow into to make it uncurl with a tiny bleat of sound. She blew it at Herb.

He ducked. "All right, but people don't face reality. Including us. They don't know what's happening out there." He left the kitchen.

"He's upset about his uncle," Margaret said. "He pretends it's other things botherin' him."

Annah licked a crumb of frosting from one of the candles. She didn't want to think about depressing things. She loved this big, warm kitchen, where Margaret kept everything spic and span and made good things to eat and always had time to comfort a kid. "It was a wonderful party, Margaret. The best ever."

Margaret was still thinking about Uncle Herbert. With her soapy hand she pushed the hair away from her forehead. "He was older than your father, and I never thought they was so close, but a loss is a loss."

Annah thought of the twenty-second floor and shivered. "I'm scared even to look out the window that high up. How could things have been so bad that he'd *jump*?" She stood with her back to the big black iron range to feel the warmth.

"Brokers mess around with other people's money. That's their job. I guess he lost it. Maybe it's best to be poor after all. Not so dangerous."

Annah wanted to tell her father how sorry she was, but he had already left for Boston "to see to things."

Later, in her pajamas, she wrapped the quilt around her and knelt by the open window. The bare branches of the elms made black lacy patterns against the blue-black sky. She could almost hear Uncle Herbert's light voice saying, "Say, you've grown a foot, Annah." He always said it, and it was a joke, because Annah was still only five feet one. Now he would never say it again. The familiar voice was gone the way the wind goes. The goofy little grin was gone, and the squared-off shoulders. She tried to think of Uncle Herbert as a spirit, a soul, but she couldn't make it work.

She sighed and got into her four-poster bed. The walls of her round room curved about her like comforting arms. On the ceiling, when she looked up, she saw the silver star that her father had pasted up there one time when she was sick in bed for a week. On her beloved Queen Anne dresser, which her grandmother had given her, were pictures of the family: her mother and father at their wedding; Herb and herself as babies and then toddlers; her class picture last year; Richie sitting on his bike and making faces at the camera. This room, these things, were real. She had thought of them as part of who she was, the background she lived and moved in, that would last forever. But things happened. People could die. People could lose all they had. Even her own family, even Margaret. Or herself. She pulled the pillow close around her face and tried to stop thinking.

CHAPTER 2

HE MORNING after Uncle Herbert's funeral, Annah met Tillie and Betsy at the train station at seven-thirty, the same as usual. Although their other friends went to the local school, these three went to a private day school in Salem. It was a small school, only six girls in the ninth grade. Annah liked it; she was serious about school. She had been enrolled at Wellesley since the year she was born, and was determined to pass her college boards and get in. She was counting on Wellesley to turn her into the successful writer she intended to be.

"Hi. What do you know?" Tillie yawned. She said the same thing every morning.

"Not much." It was too early to be original and witty.

Betsy was hanging around the boy who sold the morning papers to the commuters. She always flirted with him. It made Annah nervous this morning, because there had been sensational headlines in the papers about Uncle Herbert. STOCKBROKER HURLS SELF 22 FLOORS. PROMINENT BROKER PLUNGES TO HIS DEATH. But already other news had replaced Uncle Herbert. There would probably be a story on the financial page, but nowhere else.

The crossing bells rang, and the gate tender came out to lower the gates. The train chugged in, spitting cinders and smoke. The smell of soft coal made Annah's throat smart. Commuters came out of the waiting room. Annah and her friends moved to the car where their favorite brakeman, Ernest, was. He said good morning and helped them up the high iron steps, squeezing their elbows a little. Annah used to think he squeezed only hers. When she found out he did it to Betsy and Tillie, too, it had been disillusioning.

As they settled into their favorite dusty green plush seats, Betsy said, "Well, how was the funeral?"

"Betsy!" Tillie was shocked. "You think it was a party or something?"

"I was just politely asking." Betsy put on her innocent look.

"It was a funeral, that's all." Annah didn't want to talk about it. It had been in the Old North Church, and there had been a lot of flowers, but hardly anyone came. Her father's and Uncle Herbert's mother and brother lived in Chicago, too far to come on the train on short notice, or so they said. Uncle Herbert had never married, never really made friends or done much of anything except play golf and make money. It seemed very sad to Annah.

Betsy announced that she and her mother were going to New York over the weekend to buy clothes, and while Betsy and Tillie were arguing about clothes, they were plunged into the darkness of the Salem tunnel. When they came out on the other side, Tillie was asking Annah if she would trade one of her lunch sandwiches for a ham and cheese.

"I just hope they can make the cocoa today without that awful scum on top," Betsy said.

As they walked from the station to school, up Chestnut Street, Annah felt very conscious of how life went on just as before. The stately Federal houses built by sea captains a century ago lined the street, protected by the big trees. It was one of Annah's favorite streets, and it hadn't changed in a hundred years. But think of the people who had come and lived and died!

At school her friends were tactful about her absence. No one mentioned Uncle Herbert. In fact all of them, including her teachers, were so gentle with her, she began to feel as if it were she herself who had been wiped out.

But gradually the world righted itself. Later when she looked back at her diary leading up to Thanksgiving, her life sounded as if it would never change. School went on as before; on Friday nights she went to dancing school in the Unitarian parish house, as she had done since she was six. Richie reached his fourteenth birthday and had a party. And in Annah's class they did *Le Chevalier de Blanchefleur* in French, with Annah playing Blanchefleur. The mothers came, and everyone praised her accent.

A few days before Thanksgiving, Herb came home from Hanover. Uncle Herb had been the only relative near enough to share holidays with them. This year it would seem strange without him. Annah's grandparents in Florida called, as they did around the big holidays, and Grandpa Bennett bragged about his orange trees, as he always did. Annah's father called his mother in Chicago, but he phoned from his office. He said she sounded sad about Uncle Herb.

The afternoon before Thanksgiving, Aunt Edna called from New Hampshire. She was Annah's mother's younger sister. She was living alone in the cottage on the lake, where Annah and her family sometimes spent a week or two in summer. After Uncle Joe had been killed in a train wreck in Spain, Aunt Edna had come home to the States and moved into the cottage. She had had it winterized, weather stripped, storm windows put on, and a Franklin stove installed in the fireplace so she could stand the winters.

"It must be awfully lonesome in the winter," Annah said.

"She goes over to town nearly every day," Herb said. "I think it would be swell. You ought to go visit her, Sis."

"Not me. I'll wait for summer." Aunt Edna didn't even have running water. She had a well and a pump in the kitchen sink. And if she wanted to telephone, she had to snowshoe across the lake to the public phone outside the drugstore. Annah pictured her standing there in the bitter cold, probably nobody around on Thanksgiving eve. It must be hard for her, Aunt Ed who had always had such a glamorous life.

Her mother thrust the phone at her. "Here, talk to Edna. Hurry, it's expensive."

"Hello, Annah." Aunt Edna had a low, musical voice, like an actress, like Katharine Cornell, who was Annah's favorite. "Are you having a nice time with Herb home?"

"Wonderful." There was a lot of noise on the line. In her mind Annah pictured the telephone poles sticking up in the dark sky all the way to New Hampshire. "How are you, Aunt Ed?"

"Fine. It's beautiful up here now. Everything's covered with rime frost. It's a silver world. I wish you were here; we'd go skating."

"Sounds great. How are Henry and Alice?"

Henry was Aunt Edna's elderly Welsh terrier. Alice was a Manx cat who had adopted Aunt Edna.

"They're fine. We're going to share a turkey tomorrow. It's snug and warm with the Franklin stove. Joe Turner caught me some trout for breakfast. I wish you were here."

For a moment Annah wished she were, too. It sounded nice. But only for a few days, not all the time, the way Aunt Edna was doing it now. After she hung up, she felt sad. Aunt Edna sounded cheerful, but that was probably so they wouldn't worry about her. She must be lonely, up there all by herself, without even any neighbors in the winter. She and Uncle Joe had led such a wonderful life, traveling all over the world. A New Hampshire lake in winter must seem pretty bleak.

Later, when Annah and her mother and brother were having dinner, not waiting for their father, who often missed the train and had to wait till nine, Annah said, "Poor Aunt Ed."

"She could live with us as well as not," her mother said. "She could have the whole third floor now that Herbert is at college."

"Mother," Herb said, "you know she never will."

"She's so stubborn."

"If I were Aunt Edna," Annah said, "I'd live in Paris or Rome or somewhere, the way she and Uncle Joe used to."

"My poli-sci prof says they're going to have a war over there," Herb said.

"Oh, Herbert," his mother said, "you're always so gloomy."

He rolled his eyes. "That's right, Mother. There won't be a war. And we don't have a depression. And all is for the best in this best of all possible worlds."

"I think it's Dartmouth that makes you so depressing," she said, as if, Annah thought, he had contracted a cold or something. "It's such a desolate place."

Herb laughed and shook his head. "You live in a little golden world all your own, Mother. With a moat around it. Dad gets up and fills the moat every morning before he goes to work."

Annah laughed at the picture that flashed through her mind of her father with a watering can, filling a moat. But her mother flushed and looked hurt. She pushed the bell under her foot to summon Margaret. "We're ready for dessert, Margaret," she said. "And please keep the meat and vegetables hot for Mr. Perry."

Margaret didn't say anything, but her look said, "as if I didn't know enough to do that, after all these years."

Later, Annah thought it was strange that none of them had heard her father come in. Perhaps it was because they weren't expecting him just then. He had taken the Gloucester Branch train to Beverly Farms, as he sometimes did when he missed his own, and had gotten a ride home with Perry France, who always drove to the Farms.

Suddenly, in the middle of dessert, he was standing in the doorway, still in his topcoat, his felt hat pushed back on his head.

Annah's mother looked up and said, "Charles!"

Annah was startled at his appearance. His face was haggard, and he looked twenty years older. She wondered if he had stopped with some of his friends at the speakeasy in Boston where they went sometimes. You could get bathtub gin in that place that would really make you sick.

Her mother pushed back her chair and went to him. For a moment they looked at each other, as if reading something. Then, without a word, they went into the den and closed the door.

Herb and Annah looked at each other in alarm.

Margaret came into the room and said, "Whatever's happened now?"

Half an hour later, the two were still in the den and Margaret was worrying about "the mister's dinner drying up like sawdust." Finally she put on her hat and coat and went home.

Annah went into the living room and turned on the radio. She only half-listened to the *William Tell* Overture and then a voice saying, "A fiery horse with the speed of light, a cloud of dust, and a hearty hi ho, Silver!" It was the Lone Ranger.

Herb wandered restlessly around the room. "The speed of light," he said, "is 186,000 miles per second."

Annah looked at him blankly. She thought she would scream if her parents didn't come out of the den soon and tell them what the matter was.

But they didn't come out, and after a while she went up to her room and began to do French irregular verbs. It was after nine o'clock when Herb knocked on her door. He looked almost as pale as her mother had.

18

"Get your coat," he said. "I'll buy you a hamburger at the diner." He went downstairs.

She was puzzled. If anything were really wrong, Herb wouldn't take her to the diner, would he?

She got her coat, and Herb drove them downtown in his Chrysler roadster. It was only a four-minute walk, but Herb loved to drive his car. He had the top down, and the east wind was cold.

Tony, who ran the diner, and the four men at the counter spoke to them when they came in. One of the men was the public school janitor, and the other three worked for a relief project. One of them had been in high school with Herb. His clothes were shabby, and he had the collar of his jacket turned up, as if even in here he felt the cold.

Annah looked at Herb in his gray tweed topcoat, his pressed gray flannels, his white shirt and his tie and Harris tweed jacket. The difference between Herb and Phil Sullivan made her uncomfortable. She wondered if it made Phil angry.

Herb ordered hamburgers for them, and they ate in silence for several minutes. Finally she said, "What's going on anyway? At home?"

He frowned and shook his head, glancing at the other men. Then he took a silver pen out of his pocket, wrote some words on a paper napkin, and gave it to her.

She stared at the words. DAD LOST HIS JOB. They didn't make any sense. "That's impossible," she said finally. Her voice sounded too loud.

Herb put the money for the food on the counter and grinned at Tony. "Keep 'em rolling, boy."

"Take it easy, Herb," Tony said. "Don't learn too much up there with them Eskimos."

On their way out Phil Sullivan looked at Herb and said, "How's it going?"

"Real fine." Herb sounded perfectly normal. "How about you?"

Phil made a face. "Gettin' a good set of biceps. Tote that barge, lift that bale."

Herb put his hand on his shoulder. "Save me a place," he said lightly. "I may join you."

Phil gave a dry little laugh. "Oh, sure."

When Herb and Annah were in the car again, he turned down Walnut Road, and she knew he was heading for the beach. Whenever they wanted to have a serious talk, they had always gone to the beach at all times of the year.

He was driving fast. The wind cut Annah's face, and she turned up her coat collar and slid down on the leather seat to avoid the worst of it. She liked the smell of Herb's car. But it couldn't keep her from thinking about the words he had written on the napkin. He couldn't have been serious. Their father had worked at the bank ever since he was twenty-three years old. He was one of the vice presidents now.

By the time Herb pulled off the road into the empty parking lot, she was sure he had been joking. On all the checks that the bank issued, right under the bank's name it said, SAFE AS AMERICA.

CHAPTER 3

HE SAND squeaked under their shoes. Herb was walking so fast, Annah almost had to run to keep up with him. Gray clouds scudded across the face of the moon. She wished he would slow down. It was hard to run in dry sand.

He went right to the water's edge, where the sand was wet and packed hard. The tide was coming in. He turned north and followed the foamy edge of the water, sometimes splashing through the incoming waves, till he came to a flat boulder at the edge of the sea. After boosting himself to the top, he gave Annah a hand up. The rock was cold and covered with patches of algae.

Annah stared into the velvety blackness of space that was the ocean. England was out there, if she could only see that far.

Herb took his pipe out of his pocket and tamped tobacco into it. Smoking a pipe was something he had taken up at Dartmouth. Annah liked the smell of it. Sometimes he let her take a puff or two, but tonight he didn't even look at her.

"You must have misunderstood Daddy," she said. "He couldn't lose his job."

He gave her a brief glance. "It's hard to misunderstand a man when he says, 'I got fired.'"

Her stomach seemed to flip-flop. "But why?"

"The bank is closing."

"How can it close? It's been there since 1886."

He gave a hard little laugh. "I know. Safe as America. But America doesn't seem too safe lately, does it?"

"It will open again. The bank."

He struck another match. His pipe had gone out. "That's what Mother keeps saying. Or that he'll get another job. Better, of course."

"Well, he will. People like Dad."

He made the kind of sound he always made when he thought she was being dumb. He used to say, "You're so stupid, it makes my teeth ache," but now that he was grown up, he said something that sounded like "ecch."

"Well, why not? That isn't the only bank in the world." She felt angry with him. He should have more faith in their dad.

He took a deep breath and pointed the stem of his pipe at her. "What you and Mother don't seem to get through your heads is there's a depression going on. Banks are failing, companies are going broke. Millions of people are wandering around without jobs, going hungry, people with no roof over their heads."

Annah began to tremble. Her teeth chattered. "Not us," she said. "Not us."

His voice grew gentler. "Look, kiddo, I'm not trying to scare you. I just think we have to face it. We're broke." He turned his head and stared out at the dark sea. "I'll be dropping out of college as soon as the semester ends. Maybe sooner."

"Herb! No!" One of the certainties of her life was that Herb would be at Dartmouth and she would go to Wellesley. They had been enrolled by their father as soon as they were born.

"Well, it's not the end of the world." But he sounded as if he thought it was.

"But what about Daddy's savings? I know he had quite a lot, because I heard Mother argue with him about using some of it to buy a summer house at the beach."

"Sure, he saved. Put it into stocks." Herb paused. "Uncle Herbert was his broker."

"Then why . . ." She stopped as what he had said registered. "Uncle Herbert."

"Who died without the price of a shoeshine."

"Daddy's money is all gone?"

"Every dime."

"Oh." She leaned back on her hands. The cold rock dug into her palms. "We've got the house."

"And there's no mortgage, thank God. But we can't sell it if nobody's buying. And nobody is."

She sat up straight. Her heart began to pound. "Sell it! Nobody's thinking about selling our *house,* are they?" The house was the family. It was who they were.

"People don't necessarily stay in one house forever."

But this wasn't 'forever'; this was now. "Where would we go?"

"Nobody's got that far yet. I'll be gone. Maybe you could stay a while with the grandparents. Or Aunt Edna." Then, seeing her shocked face, he said, "Well, don't worry about things till they happen."

"What do you mean, you'll be gone?"

"I'll ride the rods. I want to go to the West coast. They say it's not quite so bad out there yet. Maybe I can get a job with the Wobblies."

It seemed to her he was talking a strange language, like Alice in Wonderland. "What are Wobblies?" Herb 'riding the rods' made her remember the tramps who came to their kitchen for a handout. How could he think of such a thing?

"It's a labor movement. It's the workman's only hope."

Herb had never worked for money a day in his life, except when his father paid him to shovel the snow in the driveway.

He turned up the collar of his coat. "Let's go. It's cold."

As they walked back to the car, Annah suddenly stopped short. "Will I have to leave my school?"

"Annah, I don't know."

She tried to imagine it. Leaving her class, her friends, Miss Shawn and Mademoiselle and her good friends. She began to cry.

Herb put his arm around her for a moment. She couldn't remember his hugging her since the time she broke her ankle skating when she was nine.

"You'll be okay. It's not you I worry about—it's Mother."

She made herself stop crying as they walked to the car. "Why do you worry about Mother?"

"I don't know if she can take it. She loves being somebody in town, having a nice house, money to spend."

When they were in the car, he took off his hat and gave it to her to hold. It had almost blown off on the way to the beach. She looked at the label. A Mallory hat. She looked at his profile and thought about how he always wore clean white Hathaway shirts and changed them two or three times a day. Sometimes it seemed as though Margaret was forever washing and ironing Herb's shirts. He sent them home from college in a square canvas laundry case. "Who will launder your shirts?" she said. But the wind tossed her words away.

"What?" he said.

"How long has Dad known about losing his job?"

"It's been rumored around for weeks. Haven't you noticed how strained he's been? The minute I got home, I saw it."

"No, I didn't notice anything."

He made a face. "Kids don't see anything except themselves."

That made her angry. "I do too notice things," she said. "And just because you've gone off to college, you're not so grown-up." She threw his hat out the side of the car, but he didn't notice.

"Dad looks ten years older," he said. "And Mother's a nervous wreck. Especially after all that disgrace stuff about Uncle Herbert."

When they got home, he said, "Where's my hat?"

"You made me mad. I threw it out."

He gave her a long look. "All right," he said. "All right." He never mentioned the hat again.

CHAPTER 4

NNAH thought she had never spent such an awful day as that Thanksgiving. The worst of it was that nobody talked about the doom that had fallen on them. Everyone seemed determined to act as if nothing had happened. Margaret had never cooked a better dinner: roast turkey, chestnut dressing, two kinds of potato, squash, turnips, cranberry relish, plum pudding, mince pie, and squash pie.

They all said things like, "Best dinner we ever had." Or, "Margaret, you outdid yourself on the plum pudding." And of course, "I ate too much." Just as if it were any ordinary Thanksgiving, instead of one where their lives were in a shambles.

Herb and her father went to the Beverly-Salem football game in the morning, the way they always had since Herb was a little boy. At dinner they talked more than usual about the game, as if it were a safe subject at least. Annah tried to smile and say things like, "That must have been exciting!" the way her mother did. But later she couldn't remember who had won the game.

While she was helping Margaret stack the dishes, a frightening thought occurred to her. "Margaret! If we don't have any more money, how can we go on having you?" She dropped a bunch of dirty forks on the floor and began to cry.

Margaret hugged her hard for a minute, and then gently pushed her away. "There, there, there, you're soaking my apron. You'll be flooding the kitchen next."

"We won't have you," Annah said.

Margaret sat Annah down on a stool and stood in front of her. "Listen now, Annah. You'll always have me, long as you want to. I couldn't love you more if you was my own."

Annah mopped her wet face. She had never before heard Margaret say she loved anyone, although she must have loved Johnny LeFaver when he was sober.

"I can't live without you," Annah said.

"Tush and nonsense." She handed Annah a clean handkerchief. "We're friends. Friends don't say good-bye when the money gives out." She began scraping the dishes into the garbage pail, what Annah's mother called "the waste" because she thought the word "garbage" was vulgar. Margaret called it "swill," but Annah was not allowed to say that.

"A lot of folks are onto hard times," Margaret went on. "They say it builds character." She gave a mocking little grin. "That's why I'm such a Rock o' Gibraltar meself. Hard times brought me to this land, a slip of a girl with not a penny to bless herself with. If your father hadn't promised me a job, if my sister Daisy hadn't pestered him till he said he would, I'd be in the old country still, or dead from starvation. But I'm here, and I'll worry when I have to, not before. You do the same."

When Annah went back to the living room, her father was sitting close to the radio, listening to Lum and Abner at the Jot 'Em Down Store and laughing as if he didn't have a care in the world. Her mother was pretending to knit. She looked white and drawn, with dark circles under her eyes. Annah would have bet money that before morning her mother would have a migraine.

Herb sat on his spine reading the sports page of yesterday's paper, which he had already read.

Usually her father turned off the radio after Lum and Abner, but this time he left it on for the next program, although the whole family hated the program. "Who's that little chatterbox? The one with pretty auburn locks? Who can it be? It's LITTLE ORPHAN ANNIE!" Annah thought she was sickening, but she took her cue from her father and laughed as if it were the greatest show on earth.

When the program changed to Kate Smith singing "We gather together to ask the Lord's blessing," Annah decided she couldn't take any more. She mumbled an excuse and went upstairs to her room.

Lying on her bed, she began to think about Aunt Edna up there in New Hampshire, "upcountry," as they said, all alone at the end of the lake, the other cottages shuttered and dark. She was so different from Annah's mother, who couldn't exist without a busy social life. When Uncle Joe was alive, they had always been off to some glamorous place on one of his photography assignments for some magazine. Uncle Joe had been a very good photographer, but they had lived "high off the hog," as her mother said, and now Aunt Edna had to be careful of her money. How did she stand it?

Later in the evening, Annah's father came in for a minute. He sat on the edge of the bed, looking out the window. "I guess Herb told you I lost my job."

"Yes. I'm sorry." She felt nervous. What was she supposed to say?

"I'm looking for another one. It may take a while." He leaned over and kissed her forehead. "Be nice to your mother."

"How do you mean?"

"Oh, I don't know." His voice broke. "Be a comfort to her. She's pretty unhappy." He looked as if he might cry.

She hugged him. "Don't worry, Dad. It'll be all right."

He gave her a sad little smile and left. It made her angry that such a disaster should happen to a man who was a hard and conscientious worker, a good father. It wasn't fair. Margaret had said, "Whoever promised us 'fair'?" but just the same, it wasn't right.

Without thinking much about it, she got her Scout knife from her desk and knelt by the windowsill, where she had carved her initials a long time ago. She'd been scolded for it then. But now was different. She wanted the world to know that this was her house, her room. Carefully she chipped out the paint that had almost obscured the A.A.P. When they were clearly visible, she folded the knife and went to bed. She didn't know exactly why, but it had made her feel a little better.

CHAPTER 5

VERY morning her father came to breakfast at the usual time, dressed in a three-piece suit, and every morning he took the eight-eleven train to Boston, as he had done for years. To a stranger it would look as if nothing had happened, but in a small town everyone knew: Charlie Perry's bank had closed; Charlie was out of a job.

Annah tried to imagine what he did in Boston all day. She knew he had appointments with people at other banks. She supposed he had lunch with old friends, listening for any rumor that might mean an opening somewhere. She read in the paper about "a line of men seven blocks long waiting for an interview for one janitorial job," and she pictured him in that line. She studied the newspaper pictures of men with blank eyes standing in line for a cup of coffee and a doughnut. She pictured him buying an apple for five cents from an old woman on the Common and having that for lunch.

She studied him secretly, looking for signs of decay. She had always thought he was handsome, with his thick black hair and blue eyes. Oddly enough, he still looked the same.

Her mother never came down to breakfast, but that was not unusual. She liked to read late at night and sleep late the next morning. Margaret could take better care of them than she could, she always said. But since her husband had lost his job, she often did not come down to lunch either. Annah would not have known it, since she was at school, but Margaret told her. She was worried.

"She's having a lot of them migraines," Margaret said.

When she did join the family, she seemed almost giddy, trying too hard to talk and laugh as she used to.

"The way we used to be" was a phrase that went through Annah's mind a lot. Even at school things were different. Betsy had promptly told everyone that Annah's father had lost his job and that Annah might have to leave school. The whole ninth grade cried. Even Miss Shawn had tears in her eyes, but she told the girls not to be so emotional. "Tears are contagious," she said. "Pull yourselves together, ladies."

After school she often rode her bicycle to favorite places, as if they might disappear overnight.

One afternoon Richie caught up with her as she leaned on the old stone bridge and stared into the sluggish stream, where they skated in winter. Weeds stuck up through the ice and tripped you, but she had liked skating upriver as far as the Hunt Club and walking home through the fields with her skates slung around her neck and the sky turning deep blue with the bare black branches of the trees etched against it.

"Remember," Richie said, "how we used to lie on our backs under the bridge and listen to the cars rumble across?"

She remembered, and it made her sad. They were talking about their childhood as if it were long ago.

"I wonder where we'll be next year at this time,"

he said. But he meant where would she be. His family had always lived in the house where his father was born, and probably always would.

The next morning the ground was white and the snow was coming down hard.

"Winter couldn't wait to get started," Margaret grumbled. "And not even Christmas yet."

Annah looked up in surprise when her father came down to breakfast. He was wearing ski pants, a sweater, and a wool shirt. Before she could ask him about it, her mother came into the room in her housecoat, looking pale without makeup, her blonde hair mussed. She didn't say good morning. Margaret and Annah watched her, uneasy at this sudden appearance.

"Why are you dressed like that?" she said to her husband.

He looked as if he had been caught doing something wrong. "I'm sorry I woke you." He gestured toward the window. "We've got a good-sized snowstorm on our hands." He looked at Annah. "The trains aren't running. No school for you today."

For a moment Annah was too pleased with that news to keep track of the conversation. Then she heard her mother say, "Are you going skiing?"

Her father laughed. "No, Myra. I just talked to Don Fuller." He paused, as if they should know what that meant.

Annah remembered that Don Fuller was the street commissioner. He was in charge of snow clearance.

"I'm going out with the snow-shovelling crew," he said. He looked hard at all three of them, as if challenging them to disapprove.

Annah's mother put out her hand for the back of

a chair without looking at it, the way old blind Mr. Jenkins did. "You're what?" Her voice sounded far away.

"I'm going to shovel snow. We need the money."

Annah's mother fainted.

Annah was amazed. She had never seen anyone faint. She would have said it was only done in novels by Dickens and books like that, but here was her mother crumpled up on the rug.

Her father and Margaret picked her up and carried her upstairs. Her father was pale.

Annah went out to the back porch and sat on the steps. The vines on the trellis that would burst forth with purple wisteria in the spring hung limp and dry. Margaret had shoveled the snow off the porch steps. The metal hooks that supported a hammock in summer had little cones of snow on them. What if she never saw the wisteria bloom again? What if she never again swung in that hammock on a lazy summer day?

Dr. Wheeler had been upstairs with her mother. She heard him coming out now with her father.

"No, it's nothing serious, not physically," he was saying. "She's got what you might call a compound fracture of her self-respect. And that can hurt, Charles, that can hurt."

Herb had said their mother felt as if she were losing her life. It was hard for him to understand that, but Annah understood it very well. She felt the same.

She went upstairs to her room. The small panes of the casement windows were almost filled up with snow. She wished she could lock the solid wooden door and never let anyone in.

CHAPTER 6

HE NEXT couple of days were full of confusion. Annah was glad she could escape by going to school. But Margaret filled her in as soon as she got home. A lot of telephoning and telegraphing was going on, Margaret said.

"To the old people in Florida. And to your father's folks in Chicago. Even your aunt up there in the woods."

"Aunt Edna? How did they get hold of her?"

Margaret gave a long shrug. "Tellygrams here and tellygrams there, and the phone ringin' off the hook."

Annah's parents had long conversations behind closed doors, and sometimes there were sounds of weeping. Annah felt as if she were at a play, but so far up in the second balcony that she caught only fragments of what was going on.

On the evening of the Christmas party at dancing school, it was Richie's mother who drove them to the parish house. Usually it had been Annah's father. Annah was wearing her new white organdy with the eyelets that were edged in red, and new elbow-length white kid gloves. She tried to think about those things, not her parents. But all evening she couldn't really relax and enjoy the party, because she kept wondering if it was the last time she would be there.

Richie's mother told her, on the way home, that she looked pretty and kissed her on the cheek when she let her off. It was so unusual for Richie's mother to be anything but snappish, Annah felt faint with alarm.

Her father was waiting up for her. He seemed nervous. The fire was burning low in the fireplace, and two bridge lamps were turned on, but the big room looked shadowy. The tick of the grandfather clock in the hall sounded loud. She knew he was going to tell her something she didn't want to hear.

She kicked off her shoes and sat on the edge of the sofa, waiting, tensed, for whatever was coming.

"Well," he said, and cleared his throat. "I wanted to tell you. Your mother is going to visit your grandma and grandpa for a while. It will do her a world of good. She's had a lot of strain lately." He was talking fast.

Annah interrupted him. "She's going to Florida?"

"Till she gets to feeling better."

Annah thought about it a moment. Maybe it wasn't a bad idea. It might do her good. "How long will she be gone?"

He looked away. "I don't know, Annah. Until things get straightened out."

"Like a couple of weeks?" When he didn't answer, she went on. "Margaret can look after us. I'll help."

He cleared his throat again. She wondered if he was catching a cold. His Adam's apple jerked up and down.

"We're going to have to make arrangements," he said.

"What kind of arrangements?"

"Annah, there just aren't any jobs for me in Boston. I've looked and looked. I've been thinking about going home for a look around. Probably there's nothing there either, but I can stay with Mother. . . ."

She was confused. It had never occurred to her that he thought of Chicago as home. Home was here, wasn't it?

"I've listed the house with a couple of real estate people."

She gasped. "You're going to sell our house?"

He threw up his hands. "I have to try. In this rotten market probably nobody will buy. I can't swing the taxes and insurance. Houses aren't free, you know."

She felt as if he had accused her of something. "So what happens to me?"

He winced. "Annah, I'd give my right arm to spare you all this. All of you. Your mother and I have gone over the possibilities a hundred times. You could go to Florida with her. . . ."

Annah thought of the small, cluttered house in Boca Raton. She thought of her grandparents endlessly playing double solitaire. Her grandmother's fussiness. The Sunday dinners at the cafeteria where all the old people went, their big day out. The beach was too far to walk to, and she was scolded for seeking out the swampy river. "Loaded with cottonmouths," Grandma said. "Not safe."

"We spoke of Chicago," her father said, "but Mother isn't well."

Nobody wanted her. "I could stay with Margaret." Margaret lived in a tiny little unpainted house on the wrong side of town, but Annah didn't care. "I could stay with her and go to the public school."

He shook his head. "Margaret has a job. She just heard this afternoon. Assistant cook at the hospital. She'll live in the dorm there, with the nurses."

She tried to laugh. "Well, I guess I could jump out of a window, like Uncle Herb."

He looked as if she had struck him. "Don't ever let me hear you say such a thing again."

"It was just a joke."

After a moment he said, "There is another alternative. You could stay with Edna."

She stared at him. "Oh, sure! In a summer cabin, with nobody around but bears and moose? Just freeze to death. . . ." She stopped because she was afraid she was going to cry. She felt betrayed. They didn't care what happened to her.

Stiffly he said, "Your aunt Edna lives there quite comfortably."

"And you all think she's out of her mind."

He took a deep breath. "Annah, none of this is very pleasant for any of us. All we can do is try to make the best of it till things get better." He waited but she didn't answer. "Your mother is leaving for Florida tomorrow. . . ."

"Tomorrow!" And they hadn't even told her.

"The doctor advises it. You can go with her if you wish. Or Edna would like to have you there. I'd like to get things settled fairly soon, so think about it."

She watched him leave the room, his shoulders held stiff. She knew she had hurt his feelings. Well, he had hurt hers. Everybody was making plans, but nobody cared what happened to her. She wished Herb were there. But he wouldn't be any better. He'd talk about cooperation and gritting your teeth, as if it were a football game they had to get through.

And Margaret. Margaret of all people, not to have told her she had a new job.

She went upstairs and got into her pajamas, and then she went on up to the third floor to Herb's room. She curled up on Herb's narrow bed and stared at the room. It smelled like him, a mixture of wool and leather and that stuff he used to slick down his hair. His Dartmouth pennant hung on the wall over the bed, and on the bureau there were a couple of golf trophies. He had won the junior tournament at the United Shoe Club House one year.

She got up and looked in his closet. His old familiar red-and-black plaid Pendleton shirt hung there, and she put it on, then found the red woolen ski cap with the pom-pom. She put that on, too. It would be cold up at the lake in the middle of winter.

And Florida would be hot. That stifling, sticky heat that made you want to take a shower every few minutes. Only you couldn't because Grandpa was careful about the water supply. At least Aunt Edna wouldn't boss her around. Or maybe she would. Annah had never spent much time with her, only those visits to the cottage in summer, when Aunt Edna and Uncle Joe were just coming back from France or Spain or somewhere, or just leaving for someplace.

After a while she fell asleep. When she woke up, she knew that no matter how much she dreaded it, she would go to Aunt Edna's. It might warp her whole life, but it wouldn't be as bad as that crowded little house in Boca Raton, with everybody on her back.

CHAPTER 7

*I*T SEEMED to Annah that she was living in a nightmare. Her mother had taken the train to Florida. Herb was still at college. And Margaret and Annah and her father had to pack everything for storage before they were all gone and the house went up for sale. One day the real estate man came to look over the house, criticizing the old-fashioned plumbing, turning up his nose at the beautiful dark mahogany woodwork in the big living room ("People like white," he said. "Nice and cheerful, you know"), even shaking his head at Annah's room and speculating that few people would enjoy living in a round room. He found every window-pane that needed new putty, every step that needed reinforcing. He sounded, Annah said angrily to Margaret, "as if he were looking at some slum tenement."

"Well, that's how they see their job," she said soothingly. "Beat the owner down on a price, you know, then beat the buyer up . . . or however it works."

But Margaret was upset, too. Annah had found her crying over a drawerful of toys that had been Herb's and hers. She had slipped a little rag doll into her pocket, Annah's favorite doll when she was small.

Annah's mother seemed never to have thrown anything away. Deciding what to keep sometimes involved painful discussions among the three of them. In the end they packed almost everything.

Annah changed her mind a dozen times about what

to take with her. She packed and repacked her suitcases over and over.

As the rooms emptied and packing boxes stood in stacks, waiting for the moving company, the house seemed to lose its color. It was almost as if the wallpaper faded out to a drab gray, and the polished hardwood floors seemed dull. Annah felt cold all the time, although her father kept the furnace going as he always had.

At last it was the day before Annah's departure. She helped Margaret move her few things from the little room off the kitchen that she seldom used to her small house on the other side of town. Annah's father had planned to drive her, but he was delayed somewhere, so Margaret piled everything into the wheelbarrow, and they took turns trundling it across town.

Margaret's street had a row of identical unpainted houses, built at one time for workers at the mill in Ipswich. Now most of the tenants were out of jobs, and many of the houses were badly in need of repair. But Margaret's was neatly kept up.

Annah helped Margaret unload the wheelbarrow and carry the things into the house. There were four rooms, a tiny living room, a bedroom just big enough for a bed and a dresser, a small kitchen with a coal stove, and the bathroom.

"Me castle but me own," Margaret said with a grin. "Paid for."

"Why are you going to live at the hospital dorm?"

"To save my bones. It's a long way to Tipperary, as the song says, but it's longer than that from the train depot to the hospital, and most of it uphill. No, thank you, not in winter. I'll come home weekends, most likely, although my sister Rosie has a notion to rent it from me for a while, now that her hubby has skedaddled."

Annah looked around wistfully. "If you were only going to be living here, I could stay and sleep on the sofa."

Margaret looked shocked. "The banker's kid on my sofa?"

"I'm not the banker's kid anymore. I'm a child of the unemployed." She sighed. "I worry about Herb."

"Don't be worryin' about that boy. He'll land on his feet."

Annah stretched out on the old sofa that sagged at one end. A torn place had been neatly mended. "I could sleep here," she said. "I mean later, when they make you head cook at the hospital and you buy a car and live at home again. You'll need somebody to take care of the house for you. Me."

Margaret gave her a quick little pat. "Don't be always fussing in your mind about what's going to happen 'some day.' Today is enough to take care of, and don't worry, it gets to be today every single blessed mornin'. Come on, we'll take the wheelbarrow home, and I'll fix you a good supper. I made your favorite, lobster stew and johnny cake and chocolate pudding with whipped cream."

"For the last time." Annah got to her feet, although she felt as heavy as lead. "Will you be there for breakfast? My train goes at nine-twenty."

"I know that, surely. And did you think I'd let you set off for New Hampshire with no breakfast in you?" Margaret grabbed the handles of the wheelbarrow and they started down the street.

"Tillie's coming over after supper, and probably Richie."

"Well, you and Tillie can cry your eyes out and Richie can stand around looking as if he'd like to, but being a man and five feet nearly eight inches, as he's forever tellin' me, he won't be able to. It's against the rules to cry if you're over five four."

Annah laughed in spite of herself. "You're just teasing." She took the wheelbarrow from Margaret. "Let me push. I have to work up some muscles for chopping wood up north."

"Ah, you and your muscles."

"I'll write every day."

"No, you won't, so don't promise. Write when you feel like it. And you know me, the letters I write, if there are any such critters, are four lines long. Printed."

"You will write though, seriously, won't you?"

"When I can, dearie, when I can."

When they approached Annah's house, she studied it, trying to memorize every tiny detail. The mugho pines up against the front porch that she had helped her father plant. The spirea hedge that bordered the wide expanse of lawn and was always one of the first signs of spring. The lilacs that her mother had transplanted three or four times before she was satisfied. The dormer windows on the third floor that she and Herb had liked to hang out when they were small. The place above the front door that needed repainting. She swallowed tears and hurried into the house.

That night, after Tillie and she had cried on each

42

other's shoulder, as Margaret had predicted, and Richie had tried desperately to make jokes, Annah lay wide awake in bed.

"I won't forget one single thing," she murmured to the room.

In the morning, Margaret fed them heartily and said a tight-lipped good-bye. Just before they were to leave for the station, the moving van arrived. Annah couldn't bear to watch the men loading her whole life into their huge van. She went and sat in the car to wait for her father. As they finally drove to the station, she saw Betsy's mother and another woman parked across the street, watching everything. She felt as if she would explode with rage and humiliation. When Betsy's mother waved, she pretended not to see her.

At the depot the baggagemaster helped them load Annah's new bike into the baggage car. "Sorry about your bad luck, Charlie," he said.

Her father tried to grin. "It's no picnic, Jock."

"There's a lot of it going around these days."

Her father loaded her suitcases onto the rack above her seat. She could tell he was close to tears.

"It won't be for long, Dad," she said.

"You bet your life it won't." He gave her a hug so hard it hurt her ribs. "Be a good girl. Write." He turned away.

"Bye, Dad." She couldn't believe she was saying good-bye to her own father.

He gave her an anguished look and swung off the train. She watched out the window, but he didn't look back.

As the train was getting up steam, just as the brakeman called, "All aboard! All a-booord, Ipswich, Newburyport, Portsmouth . . . ," she saw Richie running down the station platform, clutching a bunch of flowers. She tried to open the window, but it was stuck shut. She ran to the door, but the train was picking up speed, and the brakeman came through in a blast of cold air, bumping into her.

"Oops. Better sit down, dear," he said.

Back in her seat, she pressed her face to the cold glass. Richie was still running, flailing his left arm the way he always did, but he was getting smaller. Then he stopped and stood still, watching the train leave, his overcoat flapping open, the flowers clutched in his hand.

CHAPTER 8

ANNAH was the only passenger left in the car. At Portsmouth when she had changed trains, there were two others, a man with a salesman's sample case and a woman who slept all the way to Rochester, where she suddenly awoke and got off. The salesman had gone to the smoking car. He came back smelling like cigars and got off at Dover.

The train was slowing down. They had passed the lake at Milton, frozen solid. If hell were cold, she thought, it would look like that. And the lake at Aunt Edna's was going to be just as frozen and desolate and empty.

Steam clouded the windows. She wiped a small place clear so she could see out. At a crossing, the big man who was tending the gates waved. She waved back, although she knew he probably didn't see her. He was bundled up in a big mackinaw and stocking cap and heavy gloves. Annah pulled Herb's ski cap farther down around her ears.

The engineer blew the whistle. It sounded thin and eerie in the cold air.

She wondered how Aunt Edna was going to get everything to the cottage. She didn't have a car. In summer she would come in the rowboat. What about the bike? Maybe she shouldn't have brought it.

There were tracks on both sides of them now. Lovell was a rail center. There were always trains standing in the station and men in gray striped overalls and tall peaked caps switching engines and doing things to the cars. She and Herb used to watch them when they were little. Suddenly she missed Herb so much it made her stomach feel hollow.

The conductor got her bags down. She buttoned up her coat and followed him to the platform between the cars as the train jerked to a stop. The air was so sharp, it hurt her lungs. Aunt Edna didn't seem to be anywhere on the platform. What if she hadn't come? Maybe she misunderstood about the time.

The train stopped with a lurch, and the brakeman jumped off and helped her down. What if her bike hadn't been transferred at Portsmouth? Where was Aunt Edna?

Just as she was beginning to feel real panic, Aunt Edna appeared, smiling and serene, as if this were an ordinary visit. She was small and pretty, and she looked young in her ski pants and parka, her cheeks red from the cold. She hugged Annah.

"Welcome to the frozen north."

Annah told her about the bike, and in no time she had found the baggageman and gotten it. Burly Billy Fraser, who delivered groceries in an old outboard in the summer, shook Annah's hand, scooped up the suitcases and the bike, and led them to a Buick touring car that must have been ten years old. He piled the luggage on the front seat and tied the bike to the running board behind a metal guard, and she and Aunt Edna sat in back.

Minutes later, they were bumping across the road onto the lake. Annah gasped. "Won't we fall through the ice?"

Aunt Edna smiled and shook her head. "No. It's about five or six feet thick. People drive on it all winter."

Annah could hardly believe it. All around the lake as far as she could see, snow was piled high, and the tall pines bent under their load. The mountains in the near distance looked like frosted cakes. The car bounced and skidded across the crusty snow that covered the ice.

Aunt Edna patted her mittened hand. "How do you like it?"

"I can't believe it!" She still felt nervous. "We're right on top of the lake!"

Aunt Edna laughed. "Now you know how Jesus felt when He walked on water."

Annah laughed, and then felt terrible. How could she laugh at a situation like this? Her life might as well be over. She was trapped in the frozen north. She stared through the blurry isinglass window curtain at the endless stretch of ice and snow. It was hopeless.

CHAPTER 9

CLUTCHING the edge of the seat as the old Buick bumped and jolted across the lake, chains clanking and rear end skidding wildly, Annah thought of the last ride she had taken the summer before Uncle Joe died. He had just bought a sleek Marmon roadster that went like the wind. Aunt Edna, who had never learned to drive, sold it after Joe's death. Annah wondered if she was sorry.

It was bitter cold. The loose side curtains flapped. Annah clenched her teeth and tried to make polite answers to Billy's friendly questions.

She was glad to hear from Aunt Edna that there was a new chemical toilet. It was bad enough stumbling down the path to the woods to the outhouse in warm weather. In winter it would be awful.

"The bathtub isn't functional in the usual way," Aunt Edna said, "but I just heat water on the stove and dump it in. The pipes are in, so you can let it drain out. Works fine."

Annah tried not to remember how inky dark the cottage was, there in the pines, once the oil lamps were blown out for the night. The dense woods came right down around the cottage, and there were wild animals out there. Bears and moose and who knew what.

After what seemed a very long time, she saw a vague landmark that was familiar. It was the island near the point where the shore swung around to the east. The lake, narrower here, went on for another half mile. The island was not far from the cottage. It looked like a white blur, the trees hung with snow. She had always been afraid of the island. A family named Sproul had a summer cottage there, hidden by the trees, and the Sprouls had a crazy son, a big boy who crashed around through the woods like a moose.

"I guess the Sprouls aren't on the island in the winter?" she said to her aunt.

"Once in a great while they come up for a weekend, but mostly not. There's really nobody on the lake at all except me." Aunt Edna smiled at Annah. "And now you."

She remembered her mother saying, "It's not safe for Edna to be there alone. Not even a telephone. What if something happened?" They didn't think much about that when they sent me up here, she thought grimly.

"I wonder what they do with Crazy Albert in the winter," Annah said.

"They have him in a school." After a minute Aunt Edna added, "I hate to hear people call him Crazy Albert. He's quite a musician and a nice boy. We're all crazy to some extent."

That seemed like an odd thing to say. Annah felt miserable and deserted and scared, but she didn't feel crazy. She kept her eyes on the island as it grew bigger in the late afternoon light. She remembered how terrified she had been once, several years ago, when she and Herb went over there. Herb had dared her to go. They had just beached the old rowboat and started to explore when Albert came crashing through the underbrush, talking to himself in a loud voice. He looked enormous.

Even Herb was scared. Albert didn't see them, but they scrambled into the boat and got out of there in record time. Afterward Herb insisted that he hadn't been scared.

She peered ahead, trying to see the cottage through the snow-crusted windshield. She could see the dock that Uncle Joe had built the summer before he died.

"Where's the rowboat?" she said.

"Stashed away under the house with the canoe."

It was getting dark quickly now. The outline of the cottage was barely visible.

"Have you seen any bears?" Annah shivered.

"They're denned up now, but they'll come begging for a handout in the spring."

Billy bumped and skidded the Buick right up to the dock, as if he were landing a boat. Annah heard Henry barking.

"Henry gets so mad when I don't take him," Aunt Edna said.

Billy left the engine running so he wouldn't have trouble starting up again after he carried the suitcases and the bike up to the porch. "No, ma'am," he said, to Aunt Edna's invitation, "thank you kindly, I won't come in. Better get this old crate into home cove before the wheels freeze to the ice." Aunt Edna tried to pay him, but he wouldn't hear of it. By the time she and Annah had climbed the wide porch steps, Billy was skidding off across the lake.

The porch looked cold and strange without the wicker furniture and the hammock. Henry was barking wildly and jumping against the inside of the door.

"Hush, Henry, hush. We're coming." Aunt Edna threw open the door and Henry leaped into her arms.

"Silly dog. Say hello to Annah while I get the lamps lighted."

Annah stood just inside the door, her hands and feet numb with cold, dodging Henry's enthusiastic kisses. She had never felt so alone in her life.

A yellow pool of light appeared on the table, lighting up Aunt Edna's head like a halo for a moment. She struck another match and lit the hanging lamp with the Tiffany shade.

"It'll warm up in a minute," she said. She was adjusting the dampers on the Franklin stove that had been installed in the fireplace. She added wood and lit the kindling. "I never dare leave much of a fire when I'm away. It's too risky. Come stand by the fire, dear. You look frozen."

As her eyes got used to the light, Annah saw something in the corner by the kitchen.

"A Christmas tree!" she said. She had hardly even thought of Christmas.

It was a beautiful tree that reached the ceiling, hung with silver and red balls and tinsel and a star at the top. A pile of wrapped presents lay on the floor beneath the branches.

"You like it?" Aunt Edna sounded almost shy.

"It's beautiful." Annah's voice broke, and she had to swallow hard to keep from bursting into tears.

In a quiet voice Aunt Edna said, "Merry Christmas, dear."

CHAPTER 10

NNAH woke in the middle of the night and couldn't remember where she was. The room was the wrong shape, and the shadows were wrong. It was very cold. Something heavy lay across her legs. For a second she felt panicky. Then Alice, the cat, moved off her legs, and Annah remembered. She was in the big attic room with its open rafters and the windows facing the lake. Cold moonlight threw shadows and made the other two beds and the bureaus and chairs look unfamiliar and almost menacing.

The hot water bottle Aunt Edna had given her was an icy blob on her feet. Her legs were cramped, and her feet were cold. She remembered too well now: Everything was gone. Her family was scattered all over the country, her house was empty and for sale. Her friends were far away. Life hardly seemed worth living.

When she woke again, it was morning and still nearly dark. The cat sat up and stretched, staring past Annah's head at the wall. Annah reached out and patted the thick orange coat, and Alice slowly moved her head and stared at Annah with her green eyes. A cat, Annah thought, will never come right out and say she's glad to see you.

She pulled the quilt up to her neck and looked around. She saw the outline of the big photograph of a moose drinking in a lake that Uncle Joe had taken, and framed with strips of birch bark. Her father said that killed the tree, but he didn't say so to Uncle Joe.

Uncle Joe had been big and handsome, with a hearty laugh. He and Aunt Edna always seemed to have a good time together, even during times when they were short of money.

Aunt Edna was already up. The smell of wood smoke and frying bacon and percolating coffee came from downstairs, and Annah realized that she was very hungry. When she swung her feet out of bed, they reached an ice-cold floor. She dressed fast.

The fire was burning in the Franklin stove, but the living room was still cool. Two bedrooms led off the living room, separated from it by curtains instead of doors, "portieres," her mother called them.

The kitchen felt warm and steamy. Aunt Edna was turning bacon with one hand and holding a full coffee cup with the other. She looked up and smiled.

"Morning. How'd you sleep?"

"Like a log. Can I help?"

"You might set the table, if you will."

Annah got the silverware and the plates with flowers on them and put them on the round oak table by the stove. In summer they ate on the screened-in porch, off the kitchen, but that was boarded up for winter. The big icebox was out there.

"What do the icemen do in the winter?" Annah asked.

Aunt Edna smiled. "Some of them work hard, cutting ice from the lake and storing it in the icehouse. If you're thinking of our iceman, young George, he goes back to college. He's a football player."

Annah thought about the handsome George for a moment. Then she thought about how profitable it must be to be an iceman in Florida. About now her mother would be getting up; no sleeping late with Grandpa banging around the house. He got up before dawn. They'd be squeezing the oranges from the trees in the backyard.

Aunt Edna poured some pineapple juice into two glasses and gave them to Annah. A moment later she brought a platter of bacon and eggs to the table and took some toast out of the ancient wire toaster that sat on the stove. She put another piece of kindling into the stove and sat down at the table. "There," she said.

"You must have been up a long time." Annah looked at the pies cooling on the work table. There were jars of cranberry relish, and loaves of bread cooling. Who was going to eat all that food?

As if answering her, Aunt Edna said, "After we clean up here, I thought you might go with me to take those things to the church. They're having a Christmas dinner for some of the poor families."

"How do you get to town without a car or anything?"

"Snowshoes."

"Oh. I should have brought my skis, I guess, instead of my bike."

"We have snowshoes. And you'll be glad of the bike later."

Henry put his chin on Annah's knee, politely begging. She slipped him a piece of toast. Alice dozed near the stove, curled up like an orange ball. Annah thought about the poor families who would eat Aunt Edna's food. Her own family was poor, but not poor enough to have to go to the church for a free dinner. Apparently there were degrees of poorness.

54

It was three days till Christmas, and she did not want to think about it. How would her mother spend Christmas? She would miss the woman who marcelled her hair. She would miss the Christmas party her bridge club always had. And what would her father do? Would he get a tree for Granny Rose? Probably not. She herself had not done any Christmas shopping, had hardly realized that it was time. She had nothing for Aunt Edna.

Would Herb spend Christmas at college? It would be deserted. People went home for Christmas vacation.

After they had washed the dishes, she put on her heavy ski pants, two sweaters, Herb's flannel shirt, her Navy pea jacket, waterproof storm boots, and Herb's stocking cap. She felt top-heavy.

She and Aunt Edna packed the pies and bread and relish into boxes and loaded the big sled. Aunt Edna found a pair of snowshoes for Annah. They were too big, and she was not used to snowshoes. She kept stepping on one with the edge of the other. Once she fell flat on the hard crust of the lake.

Halfway across the lake it occurred to her that she would have to make this trip five times a week to get to school. The thought appalled her. She stopped short, her breath coming in gasps.

Aunt Edna waited for her. "It's surprising how fast you get used to it. I walk over to town nearly every day in all kinds of weather, as long as the lake is frozen." She leaned down and retied the thong of Annah's left snowshoe. "It gets to be an adventure."

It did not sound to Annah like an adventure. She thought of her morning train and Tillie and the paper boy and Ernest, the brakeman. She even felt homesick for Betsy. She wondered what Richie was doing at that moment.

When they got to town, Aunt Edna parked the sled outside the town hall and took Annah into the drugstore, on the first floor of the town hall building, to have a hot chocolate.

Annah's feet were numb with cold, but in the warmth of the store they began to tingle and get shooting pains. She clenched her teeth and tried to wiggle her toes inside her boots, as her aunt chatted with the tall, thin man who owned the drugstore.

At the church it surprised Annah how many local people seemed to be friends of Aunt Edna's. Her mother had always said that Edna was so alone up here.

"I promised Marge Turner we'd drop in a minute," Aunt Edna said when they left the church. "I thought you'd like to meet her granddaughter. She's your age."

Annah was not expecting another Tillie, or even a Betsy, but she wasn't prepared for Mabel Turner. She was a thin girl with bad teeth and an expression that seemed to say, "Give me one reason why I shouldn't hate you."

She was in the kitchen with another girl, eating mince pie. When her grandmother introduced Annah, Mabel gave Annah a hard stare and then said, "Hi," making it sound like a declaration of war.

"And this is Mabel's friend, Dodie," Mrs. Turner said.

Annah glanced at Dodie, but Mabel was taking up so much room in the kitchen, it seemed, Dodie was hardly visible. As soon as Mrs. Turner had given Annah a piece of pie and left them alone, Mabel looked at

Dodie, jerked her head in Annah's direction, and said, "Summer people."

Dodie looked down at her hands.

"I'm not summer people anymore," Annah said. "I'm year-round."

"You don't live here." Mabel's voice dripped scorn.

Without looking up, Dodie said softly, "She does now."

"She does not," Mabel said. "She lives down the lake."

Annah felt angry and discouraged. She wondered if everybody in town was going to take this attitude. "People who live on the lake are not lepers," she said. "They don't have bubonic plague."

"Snobs," Mabel said. "Outsiders."

"I don't think so," Dodie said.

Annah really looked at her for the first time. She had a thin face with dark brown eyes that looked hungry, not just for food but for other things. She gave Annah a small, shy smile.

Mabel frowned. "You'd better run along home now, Dodie," she said as if she were speaking to a child. "Tell your father he can get you all a free meal at the church. This person . . ." Again she jerked her head toward Annah. ". . . and her aunt have just left some food at the church. At least I heard they were going to. Lots of people have. For the poor." She put a slight emphasis on the word "poor."

Dodie's face flushed bright red, but she shoved back her chair and got to her feet. Pulling her thin cotton jacket tight around her, she left the room, letting in a blast of cold air.

"That was a rotten thing to say," Annah said. She pushed away the mince pie, half eaten.

"What business is it of yours?" Mabel said. She grabbed Annah's plate and scraped the remains of the slice of pie into the garbage pail. "My grandmother won't appreciate you throwing away her good pie."

"I didn't throw it away. You did," Annah said and stood up.

Three doors led out of the kitchen, one to the back porch, where Dodie had gone out, one to the front of the house, and another that Annah guessed was a pantry. She wasn't sure which door was the one to the front of the house. She hesitated, trying to remember. It wouldn't do to march into the pantry or maybe fall down the cellar stairs if that was where the door led. Mabel stood watching her, grinning as if she had just won a battle.

Aunt Edna saved the day by appearing in the right doorway and saying, "Time to go, Annah."

As she and Annah walked down the street with their snowshoes over their shoulders, Aunt Edna said, "How did it go? Did you and the girls hit it off?"

"Fine," Annah said. The Turners were Aunt Edna's friends.

Aunt Edna gave her a quick look, but she didn't say anything.

They stopped at the railway freight office so Aunt Edna could get a box she was expecting, though she didn't say what it was.

Annah didn't have much to say on the way home. She felt too depressed to talk. Later she wrote long letters to Tillie and Richie and Margaret, and short ones to her parents. She felt like unloading her homesick-ness and worries onto Margaret especially, but she tried not to. Margaret had problems of her own, with a new job and new living quarters. Margaret's own house was still there, though, and she could go to it weekends. There was no big FOR SALE sign in front of it.

Aunt Edna cooked steaks and then wound up the Victrola so they could listen to carols on her Red Seal records. The carols made Annah want to cry. She thought about people all over the world, listening to those same carols. Some were happy, some were sad, some were comfortable and some were probably wondering if they'd have anything to eat on Christmas day. She thought of that girl, Dodie. Poor had always seemed to be people like the tramps who came to the house, and the apple ladies on the Common, and the long lines of grim-looking men lined up in Boston for a free cup of coffee. But now, "poor" was a word with a lot of different meanings.

She managed to say "Merry Christmas" to Aunt Edna before she went to bed, but merry was not how she felt.

CHAPTER 11

N CHRISTMAS morning Annah woke to a record on the Victrola playing "God Rest Ye Merry, Gentlemen." Henry came pattering upstairs and jumped on the bed.

When she came downstairs, she was surprised to see a lot of packages under the Christmas tree. She had bought a box of Aunt Edna's favorite chocolate-covered cherries the day before, while Aunt Edna was talking to her friend the postmistress, but otherwise she had no gifts for anyone.

She tried to explain to Aunt Edna.

"Most of those packages came from your family," Aunt Edna said. "They were in that big box that came by Railway Express."

"But they don't have any money."

"Your dad said these were things they bought a month or two ago. You know how your mother is about shopping early."

Annah knelt down to look at the tags. Besides the ones from her parents, there was one from Margaret, one from Tillie, one from Richie. "I didn't get anybody anything."

"My dear, they understand. People who love you don't give a present to get one back. Come eat your breakfast. I made spider johnnycake."

"Spider johnnycake" was a special kind of corn bread made on top of the stove in a big frying pan called a "spider." It was Annah's favorite breakfast. There was bacon too, and hot chocolate. The kitchen was warm, and the cottage smelled of Christmas tree.

"I don't suppose they have Christmas trees in Florida," she said.

"We'll call your mother later and you can ask her."

Thinking about talking to her mother made her feel odd. Since she had left home, it was as if her whole family had come to an end somehow, disappeared in a puff of smoke.

After breakfast Annah chopped a pile of kindling for Aunt Edna. She was getting pretty good at chopping wood. At first she was afraid she would chop her own leg off.

When she came in, they sat down to open presents.

Annah jumped up again. "Wait a sec." She ran upstairs and got the box of chocolate cherries. It wasn't much of a present. She wished she had given it more thought.

She opened her presents slowly, as she liked to do, smoothing out the ribbon and the paper before she actually opened the box. Her parents had given her new shoe skates. Richie gave her a pale blue blouse, and Tillie gave her a wool scarf that would be very useful on her long cold walks to school.

"You open one," she said. "I've been hogging all the packages." She had saved Margaret's and Aunt Edna's. On a lower branch of the tree were the envelopes from the grandparents. They had sent checks ever since Annah and Herb were past the age of four or five.

Aunt Edna had a lot of good presents from the family and from Uncle Joe's sister and from friends.

The one that intrigued Annah most was a small bottle of Chanel Number 5 from an old friend in Paris. It smelled to Annah like the ultimate in sophistication. She looked at Aunt Edna with new eyes, trying to picture her in that background. "Do you miss it?" she said.

"Miss what?"

"France and all that."

For a moment Aunt Edna looked sad. Then she laughed. *"Sic transit gloria mundi.* Or as your uncle Joe used to translate it, 'There goes old Gloria, skittering down the road with her slip showing.'"

Annah wasn't sure what that meant exactly, but she was touched that Aunt Ed had mentioned Uncle Joe. Most of the time she didn't, as if he were a secret only she knew.

She opened her present from Margaret. It was a gray flannel skirt, handmade, with pockets and everything just the way Annah liked it. She almost cried, thinking of the work Margaret had put into it. Margaret was not fond of sewing, though she did it well.

Aunt Edna gave her a package that said, "To Annah from Aunt Edna with love."

Annah opened it carefully, folding the wrapping paper. "Oh, how pretty!" The package held a handknit sweater, dark red with her monogram in a lighter shade, and matching red mittens and cap. The mittens had tiny flowers embroidered on their backs. Annah put on the cap and the mittens at once and held up the sweater to her shoulders. "They're beautiful! Handknit! Oh, I wish I could show Tillie! Well, some day I will." She got up and hugged Aunt Edna, then picked up the package of chocolate-covered cherries. "What I got you

62

is so dumb, I hate to give it to you. I just didn't do anything about Christmas at all. I feel bad about it."

Only Aunt Edna could make a seventy-cent box of chocolates seem like the one gift she had longed for all her life. "It's my favorite! Oh, what sinful joy! I shall stuff myself."

They both had one, and as Annah sat there amid the debris of wrapping paper and ribbon, licking the sticky candy from her fingers, she thought how very strange life was. If anyone had told her last Christmas that she would be here, like this . . .

Henry and Alice were playing a game with a piece of red twine. A squirrel raced noisily on the roof. The smell of roasting turkey was making Annah hungry again.

"They were wonderful presents," she said. But she was in New Hampshire and her family was scattered all over. She wanted to rush out of the cottage and walk and walk till she was tired out.

And at that moment someone knocked on the door.

"It must be the Turners," Aunt Edna said, "or perhaps Charlotte."

"I'll get it." Annah jumped to her feet. She opened the door, prepared to say "Merry Christmas" to one of Aunt Edna's friends from town. Instead she gasped and then shrieked, "Herb!"

Her brother stood there grinning, looking half-frozen, Christmas packages sticking out of his pockets. She had never been so glad to see anyone in her life.

CHAPTER 12

ANNAH was so glad to see Herb, she couldn't stop giggling. "Where did you get that sunburn?"

"My roommate and I've been skiing. Three days of it. But it's probably the last I'll get for a while."

"Did you come on the train?"

"I hitched a ride with Rob. In my own car." He grinned. "I sold him my car. I really soaked him. But he's too rich for his own good."

She was dismayed. "You sold your lovely car!"

He waved away her protest. "When you hit the road, kid, you don't usually take your own car. Do you know what gas costs now?" He was drinking the coffee Aunt Edna brought him.

When he finished, he gave them their presents, a box of bath powder for Aunt Edna. "I researched the brands," he said. "I remember how good you used to smell when you came to say good night to us when we were little kids."

Aunt Edna's eyes filled with tears. "That was a long time ago, Herbie." She covered her emotion by bending her face over the powder. "This is wonderful."

Annah thought at first that her gift was a wristwatch, but it turned out to be a compass that she could wear.

"So you won't get lost on the way to school," he said. He buckled the strap around her wrist. "Now you'll always know where true north is."

"I didn't get you anything," Annah said. "Or anybody."

"That's all right, kid. It was an unusual Christmas." He put his finger under the handsome tie he was wearing. "Thanks, Aunt Edna. You always know my type." To Annah he said, "It's from Sulka's. Just like Uncle Herb's. We may go down in defeat, but we go down in style."

After the good turkey dinner, they snowshoed to the village and made their telephone calls, first to Annah's mother, then to her father, with quick conversations with the grandparents. Granny Rose cried. Annah's mother sounded as if she were having a pretty good time. She hardly misses us at all, Annah thought. But her father sounded sad and discouraged. He had not found any work.

On the way back, Aunt Edna suggested stopping by the church to see if the people putting on the dinner needed any help. Annah felt suddenly shy about going there, afraid of seeing that girl, Dodie. It would embarrass them both.

She was not there. About a dozen people were eating silently at the long trestle table in the parish room. Mabel Turner's grandparents were washing dishes. Aunt Edna offered to help.

"It was kind of a rush there for a while," Mr. Turner said. "I didn't realize there'd be so many." He shook his head. "Winter's a bad time to be broke."

Herb helped him take out a load of ashes from the huge stove.

"Did Dodie come?" Annah asked Mrs. Turner.

"Dodie? Yes, they came early. Well, no, I'm telling a lie: Dodie's family came, but she wasn't with them.

Mabel said something about some girl having her to dinner at her house."

"Oh, good," Annah said. She felt relieved.

Mrs. Turner frowned. "That man, Dodie's father, he was drunk already, and it wasn't even noon."

"Who's Dodie?" Aunt Edna had found a dish towel and was wiping the turkey roasters.

"Oh, she's a little friend of Mabel's," Mrs. Turner said. "They're new in town, been here about six months. He's not much good, I'm afraid. Kind of a drifter."

"Is there a mother?" Annah didn't want to be a pest, but she wanted to know about Dodie.

"Yes, there is. I heard she drinks, too. Tiny little thing, looks scared out of her wits. I've heard he beats her."

"How dreadful!" Aunt Edna said. She looked at Annah.

On the way back to the cottage, she asked Annah about Dodie.

"She was in the kitchen with Mabel Turner. She acted . . . I don't know, scared or unhappy. Or both."

"Perhaps you could invite her for supper some night," Aunt Edna said.

"Well, I don't really know her."

When they were sitting around the Franklin stove, eating turkey sandwiches and drinking—coffee for Aunt Edna and Herb, cocoa for Annah—Aunt Edna questioned Herb about his plans.

"California, here I come," he said. "This boy's going to ride the rods."

Annah had the odd feeling that Herb was almost enjoying their new poverty, as if it were an adventure.

Aunt Edna tried to talk him out of California. "Riding freights may sound romantic, Herbert, but it is very dangerous."

He laughed and said teasingly, "You speak from experience, I suppose, Aunt Ed?"

They sat up late, talking about all sorts of things, from new plans to what Herb called "the old days." Annah realized with a shock that even last Christmas already seemed like the old days, another life, far away and slightly unreal.

The next day the three of them went down to the end of the lake where the wind had blown the ice clear, and they skated for a long time. Herb built a bonfire on the ice. They toasted marshmallows and sang Christmas carols and old songs until the sun was low in the western sky.

By the time they started back to the cottage, it was nearly dark, and the air was a dead still cold. It was hard to see the snowy patches on the ice. After Annah tripped and fell flat, they put their arms around each other for balance.

As they approached the dark outline of the island, Annah stared at it fearfully. It was scary enough by day; in the dark it looked really menacing. She could picture ogres lumbering around.

Suddenly she saw a flicker of light. She gasped. "Look!"

By the time Aunt Edna and Herb turned their heads, the light was gone.

"You imagined it," Herb said. "You always were scared spitless of that island."

But she knew she had seen the light. Maybe the

Sprouls had come up for Christmas. They would have Crazy Albert with them. She shivered and tried to make the others go faster, back to the safety of the cottage.

Herb stayed with them until it was time for him to go back to Hanover to finish out his semester. The day he left, he chopped a big pile of wood, and Annah stacked it.

As he stopped to warm his bare hands, he shoved his wool cap onto the back of his head and said, "Listen, Annie, be nice to Aunt Ed, won't you."

She was surprised. "Of course I'll be nice to her."

"I worry about her. She misses Uncle Joe a lot."

"She never says so."

"Of course not. But last night after we all went to bed, I heard her crying."

His words upset Annah. Aunt Edna had seemed like one person who wasn't sad all the time.

"She insisted on giving me money to get to California. I didn't want to take it, but she wouldn't let me off the hook. She made me promise."

"I'm glad of it. People get killed riding freights." She hadn't realized that she was so worried about Herb's plans. She felt as if a load had been lifted. "What will you do when you get there?"

"Pick oranges, probably," he said cheerfully. "I want to get a job with the labor movement if I can, but it may take time. Anyway I won't freeze. They say that's a dandy climate."

As he lifted the ax, she stopped him. "Herb, take me with you."

He was so surprised, he stood unmoving, with the ax uplifted, like a picture she had seen once of Abe Lincoln. "Are you crazy?"

68

"I won't be any trouble. I could pick oranges, too."

He put down the ax and said gently, "Kiddo, I couldn't do that. You're only fourteen. Think what Dad and Mother would say. . . ."

"They don't care!" she burst out. "They don't care what happens to me."

He pulled her down beside him on the edge of the enormous boulder that stood beside the woodpile. A scraggly pine tree grew out of a crack in the rock. When she was little, Annah had thought it was a magic rock.

"You know that isn't true," he said. "You know they care. Especially Dad. He feels like he's failed us. You'll be just fine here. You couldn't have a nicer person to be with than Aunt Ed."

"I know that." Annah's voice trembled. She was determined not to cry. She stared at a woodpecker who was hammering away at the top of a pitch pine.

"And she needs you as much as you need her. Think about somebody besides yourself for a change." He put his arm around her, taking the sting out of the words. "It's time to grow up, Sis." He gave her his handkerchief, and she mopped her eyes fiercely. "You'll be all right, Annie-banany. You're a good kid." He gave her a quick hug and stood up. "Tim-ber!" He brought the ax down on a log, splitting it neatly in half.

Now that he would soon be gone, she knew how much she loved him. When your brother lived in the same house with you, he could be a pain, but when he was gone, it was lonesome. He could have protected her against all those kids at school, she thought, who were going to hate her.

CHAPTER *13*

THE NIGHT before she was to start school, Annah couldn't sleep. She went over and over in her mind the subjects she would be taking: English, American history, Latin, algebra. Aunt Edna had talked to the principal before Annah arrived. There was no point in starting French in the middle of the year, he had said; they would need to find out where she was in her work.

"Those private schools," he had said, "make a big thing of French. She's probably way ahead of the other freshmen."

"Those private schools." The principal was probably going to be hostile toward her because she'd gone to a private school and came from "away," as they said. Just like Mabel Turner, looking down their noses at her because she wasn't one of them.

She got out of bed, wrapping the quilt around her, and went to the window, leaning her elbows on the sill. There was a full moon, and for a change a cloudless sky. Even through a fold of the quilt, the windowsill felt ice-cold. The island looked close in the moonlight. Although she had looked for it, she had not seen a light there again. Maybe Herb had been right, and she had imagined it. But she didn't think so.

Tomorrow Tillie and Richie and everybody would be going back to their old schools. She had had a long letter from Tillie. Tomorrow morning she and Betsy would meet at the station; Betsy would flirt with the paper boy; the brakeman would squeeze their arms when he helped them on the train. They would argue. Betsy would show off her new clothes. And at the end of the day Richie would have to find somebody else to tell all his troubles to: How the art teacher made them paint things the way *she* saw them; how the English teacher got mad at him for forgetting what you did with semicolons. Maybe he'd tell Tillie, and they'd get to be such close friends that they wouldn't even miss her after a little while. Her eyes filled with tears of self-pity.

She lit the lamp beside her bed, and got back under the covers, taking with her the blank book that Herb had given her for her birthday. She had not written in it yet; things had been too confused. It was such a beautiful book, she wanted to write worthwhile things in it.

In her small, neat handwriting, she wrote: "January 2, 1932: A new year is like a new penny fresh from the mint, shiny and clean and promising to buy you something." She read over the words. Would Miss Shawn think that was a good simile? Had she really made it up or had she read it somewhere? She was always afraid she would use somebody else's words or ideas without knowing it.

She chewed on the end of her pencil. Did Emily Brontë cross out words and rewrite a lot when she wrote *Wuthering Heights*? she wondered. Or did it just flow onto the paper? Sometimes, it seemed, she couldn't think of words that were anywhere near good enough. It was frustrating.

She bunched the pillow up behind her head and

leaned back. All she really wanted was a good English teacher. She had to work on her poetry.

The moon made a path of light across the floor and on the foot of the bed. Alice's tail flicked the light for a moment, and she looked at Annah with sleepy eyes.

"I'd like to write a poem about you," Annah said softly.

Alice blinked and went back to sleep.

It would be nice to be a cat, taking each day as it came, thinking secret thoughts and not telling anybody. It wasn't that way for her. She had this strong urge to tell what she felt, not to any particular person, not even to Tillie or Richie, but to the world. Somebody out there was bound to understand.

She thought of a quatrain she had written the first week of school, in September.

> The moon is floating
> In late afternoon
> Like a golden lily
> On a deep blue lagoon.

Miss Shawn had liked it, but she asked her if she knew exactly what a lagoon was. "Be precise," she said. Together they had looked it up. "A small, shallow pond, usually near the ocean." "So if it were shallow, it wouldn't be deep blue, would it?" Miss Shawn had said.

Annah closed her blank book and sighed. There was a lot to think about if you wanted to be a writer. Tonight's moon, for instance, was nothing like that warm September moon. It looked more like a round disc of ice in a cold sky. It was not a friendly moon.

She turned down the lamp, blew it out, and slid under the blankets. Perhaps she could write a story about her new life. She pulled Alice up against her. "I'm so scared," she said. "I'm so scared of that school."

CHAPTER 14

*T*HE HIGH SCHOOL was not big, but after the small school in Salem, which was situated in a house, it was overwhelming to Annah. There seemed to be hundreds of students. They all looked her over, and a few of the girls smiled, but nobody talked to her. She wished she were five years younger so she could stick out her tongue and say, "Like the looks?"

She was carrying Aunt Edna's snowshoes under her arm as she went into the building, and that seemed to cause some amusement. It had been cold and windy coming across the lake. She knew her face was red, and she had to keep blowing her nose, like a little kid.

She found the office and went in. Seven or eight students were trying to get the clerk's attention for one reason or another. The woman looked harassed.

"Yes?" she said to Annah, looking at her sharply.

"I'm a new student," Annah said. "Annah Perry. I live on the lake with my aunt. . . ." Her voice trailed off because the woman had stopped listening. She was flipping through a file.

After a minute she pulled out a schedule and slapped it down on the counter. "Annah Perry. There you are."

Annah picked it up and looked at it. A girl with an excused absence note began talking to the clerk.

"Uh . . . excuse me. . . ." Annah said.

"What is it?" The woman was impatient.

"They spelled my name wrong. It's Annah with an h."

The woman glanced at it. "I'll catch it later. I'm busy now."

As Annah walked away, she heard the other girl chanting softly, "I'm Annah-with-an-h, I'm Annah-with-an-h . . ."

The clerk laughed.

Annah got out of the office as quickly as she could.

A note with a combination of numbers was attached to her schedule. For a moment she didn't know what it was, but then she realized that the students had lockers. It must be her locker number and combination. She had never had a locker in her life. But maybe that would solve the problem of what to do with the snowshoes.

She made her way up to the second floor, trying not to bump into people with the snowshoes. What she was to do with them during the day had not occurred to her. If they wouldn't fit in the locker, what could she do? The thought made her stomach clench with anxiety. She'd be not only an outsider but a freak. Maybe she should have gone to Florida after all.

When she found her locker, she couldn't get it open. She tried and tried. She could feel perspiration on the back of her neck. Finally she caught the eye of the boy whose locker was next to hers. "I can't get it open." Her voice trembled, and she hated herself for being so stupid.

The boy blushed. "Oh," he said. He was a homely boy with brown hair that needed cutting, and patched corduroy pants and a jacket that looked as if it belonged to someone bigger than he was. He glanced at her combination, opened the locker easily, and fled before she could thank him.

She felt weak with relief. And if she stood them

at an angle, the snowshoes just barely fitted. She shoved her coat and cap and mittens and overshoes in around them and leaned on the metal door to close it. She was *not* going to lock it. She might never get her things out again.

She found her homeroom, and the first person she saw was Mabel Turner, sitting in the front row. Annah said "Hi," but Mabel just smirked and whispered to the girl next to her.

When the teacher had assigned her to a seat, Annah found herself across the aisle from Dodie, who gave her a shy smile and said, "Hi."

The bell rang. It sounded so loud and so close that Annah jumped and knocked her pencil to the floor. The boy who had opened her locker leaned down and picked it up for her without looking at her. She was sure he must think she was the most inept person in the whole school. But at the school she had been going to, there were no bells. The teacher just glanced at her watch at the end of the class and said, "End of class, ladies." For a minute she was so homesick for her old school her chest literally ached.

She rose hastily as the grim-faced homeroom teacher began the pledge of allegiance to the flag. After that the teacher read a few blood-curdling verses from Malachi, and visions of the damned burning like stubble raced through Annah's mind. She thought of gentle Miss Shawn reading from Song of Songs.

Her first class was history and, to her surprise, she enjoyed it. The teacher was old and small and lively, with a good sense of humor. Her glasses gleamed when she smiled. Annah got up her courage to answer a couple of questions about the American Revolution, and Mabel Turner glared at her.

Algebra was algebra. She would never be very good at math. But Latin was fun. She had already done the pages of Julius Caesar that they were working on, so she felt easy and self-confident.

Then it was noon, and there was a rush for the doors. It hadn't occurred to her that nearly everyone would go home for lunch. In no time at all the school building and grounds were deserted.

She got her lunch from her locker and looked around for some place to eat it. There was no lunch room or students' lounge, only the classrooms. She put on her coat and went outside. Luckily the sun was shining, but what was she going to do when it rained or there was a blizzard? She didn't think the authorities would be pleased if she ate in one of the classrooms.

She sat down on the wide granite steps and opened her lunch bag. After a while she was conscious of someone behind her. She turned quickly, afraid it was going to be a teacher telling her it was not allowed to eat on the steps. But it was Dodie, who sat down on the top step.

"You don't go home for lunch either?" Annah was very glad to see her. She would have been glad to see almost anyone who was not downright hostile.

Dodie shook her head. She didn't have any lunch with her, as far as Annah could see.

Annah held out a sandwich. "Want a turkey sandwich?"

"No, thanks." But Dodie looked at it as if she could hardly keep from grabbing it.

"Go ahead, take it," she said. "My aunt gives me too much. It's turkey."

Dodie hesitated. Then she reached out quickly and took it. "Thanks," she said softly. She ate it fast.

"Do you live too far to go home for lunch?" Annah said.

Again Dodie hesitated. "No. I live out by the dirt road that goes to Wolfeboro."

"How come you don't go home then?" As soon as she asked it, Annah wished that she hadn't. A look of pain crossed Dodie's face, and she flushed. "Not that it's any of my business," Annah said. "I'm glad there's somebody who doesn't, besides me. I have all I can do to get here at all, let alone go home for lunch." She knew she was chattering, but she felt bad because somehow she had embarrassed Dodie. "I live way down the lake."

"I know," Dodie said.

Annah gave her an apple, and there was a silence while they sat eating. Annah tried to think of something to say. "Have you lived here forever? I guess everybody has but me."

"Oh, no," Dodie said. "We came last year."

"Oh. Where from?"

Again Dodie looked uncertain. She stared at her hands. "My stepfather moves around a lot."

"Oh, does he work for the railroad or something?"

"He doesn't have a job."

"Oh! My father doesn't either!" It was strange to be glad she could say that. It seemed like a bond between them.

Dodie looked unbelieving. "*Your* father?" She glanced at Annah's clothes.

78

"He lost it just a few weeks ago. The bank he worked for closed."

Dodie looked thoughtful.

"My uncle lost his too, and some other people's money, I guess. He killed himself. Jumped out of a twenty-second floor window."

Dodie gasped. "How awful!"

"Yeah. My brother is going to California to pick oranges. He was going to ride the rods, but my aunt is giving him the fare so he won't get killed or anything."

"Is your aunt rich?"

"Oh, no. Uncle Joe died in a train wreck. He had insurance and some money, I guess, but not a whole lot."

Dodie finished her apple and ate most of the core. "I thought you were rich," she said.

"Not me."

After a long pause Dodie said, "I'm glad you're not."

"Why?"

"I'd like to be your friend, but I don't think I could be friends with anybody rich. They wouldn't like me anyway."

"That's crazy," Annah said. "People don't like or not like people because they're rich or not."

"Oh yes, they do," Dodie said. "Many people do."

Annah wanted to ask her questions. Maybe being poor was an art that a person could learn. She would like to know, for instance, how Dodie managed to seem dignified and self-respecting when all she had for a winter coat was a shabby cotton jacket that she pulled around herself. She wanted to ask what you did when you were hungry and there wasn't any food. She couldn't imagine herself in that situation, but she could not have imagined herself with an unemployed father a couple of months ago.

She began to worry about what would happen to Herb if he couldn't get a job picking oranges. There must be thousands of people after those jobs. Would Herb go hungry? The questions kept coming all afternoon, about how people learned to be poor.

She was still thinking about it when the dismissal bell rang. She went to her locker. Her snowshoes were gone.

CHAPTER *15*

SHE COULDN'T believe it. Everything else was there, but the snowshoes were gone. "No!" she said, and banged her hand against the metal door.

The boy at the next locker jumped. "What's the matter?"

"Somebody took my snowshoes."

The people going past her in the hall heard her. A couple of girls giggled. A boy said, "What a dirty trick." And an older girl with her blonde hair braided in a coil around her head said, "Tell them at the office."

Annah grabbed her coat and hat, mittens, and boots. Her hands were trembling. The snowshoes belonged to Uncle Joe. They were too big for her and she tripped over them, but they were *Uncle Joe's*. Aunt Edna would feel bad if they were gone.

She pushed her way through the crowd and ran down the stairs, not noticing the people she bumped into. Dodie was just going out the door, and Annah wanted to call to her, but Dodie was hurrying and didn't see her.

Half a dozen students were milling around in the office for one reason or another. She pushed past them to the desk, where the clerk was talking to an older boy.

"Somebody took my snowshoes," Annah said.

The clerk stared at her and blinked. "They what?"

"Are you sure?" the boy said.

"Of course I'm sure. You can't overlook a pair of snowshoes. They were men's size."

The girl with the blonde braid came into the office. The boy looked at her and said, "This girl's lost her snowshoes."

"I know."

"Do you know anything about it, Doris?" the clerk said.

The blonde girl looked at her. "Are you asking me if I took them, Mrs. Penner?"

The clerk looked embarrassed. "Of course not. You're president of student council, for goodness sake. I was just asking if you knew about anybody . . ." Her voice trailed off.

"If I did, I'd go get them." To Annah she said, "Where do you live?"

"Way down the lake."

"Oh, you're that one."

"Can you get home without them?" the boy asked Annah.

"Are you sure you looked in the right locker?" Mrs. Penner said.

"My hat and coat were there." Annah's burst of rage was fading, and she was struggling not to cry.

"Somebody must have been playing a joke." The blonde girl turned as another older girl came up behind her. "This girl's snowshoes disappeared out of her locker."

"Oh, good grief." The new girl was pretty, with long wavy brown hair.

"Betsy did it." One of the boys who had been listening said it and laughed a hoarse guffaw.

The new girl threw a small eraser at him. "Hush up, Johnny Fabian. I don't even know how to snow-shoe."

Betsy. A girl named Betsy here in this school. It seemed like a tremendous coincidence. Her own Betsy and the others at home flooded into her memory with such vividness she could hardly stand it. In *that* school nobody would ever steal anything or play cruel tricks.

"I'd better tell Mr. Pierce," Mrs. Penner said. She hurried on her high heels to the principal's office.

"As if he'd know," the tall boy muttered.

"Be quiet, Jamie," the blonde girl said. She turned to Annah. "My name's Doris Hay. This is Betsy Bennett and Jamie Fontaine. We're on the student council. We want to help. If the snowshoes don't turn up this after-noon, can you get home all right?"

Annah nodded miserably. She felt like leaning her head on the shoulder of this tall, efficient-sounding girl and bursting into tears. But only babies did things like that. "I can walk."

"Kind of rough going though," Jamie Fontaine said. "I could go home and get my skis and you could borrow them . . ."

"Oh, Jamie, your feet are so big, she'd fall out of your skis," Betsy said.

"All she has to do is tighten the straps . . ."

"No, thank you very much, I'll be all right. It's just that they're my aunt's snowshoes. I mean my uncle's really, only he died and . . ." It seemed too complicated to go on.

Doris patted her shoulder. "Don't worry. They'll turn up sooner or later. Somebody is playing a joke."

"Some joke," Jamie said.

Annah really looked at him for the first time. He was a very good-looking boy, with shiny dark hair that waved a little around the temples, and dark blue eyes with long lashes.

Mrs. Penner came out of the office. "Mr. Pierce will speak to you now," she said. She looked relieved, as if telling Mr. Pierce had taken the whole thing off her shoulders.

Mr. Pierce sat behind a large desk. He was so short that Annah had the feeling his feet didn't touch the floor. His black hair stood up like a brush. He looked at her over his steel-rimmed glasses. "Now then, what is all this about snowshoes?"

"They're gone."

He put the tips of his fingers together and studied them as if the secret might be there. "Did you lock your locker?"

"No. I had trouble with the lock."

"Ah! There's your problem. You should have come to Mrs. Penner and explained the problem."

"I'd have been late for class." She felt as if he were blaming her for the disappearance of the snowshoes. "I thought people in this school were honest."

He winced. "I believe this school to be entirely honest. There must be some mistake. What is your name?"

"Annah Perry." As an afterthought she said, "Annah with an h."

He pursed his mouth and then allowed himself a tiny smile. "And Annah-with-an-h has lost her snowshoes."

Annah tried to smile, but she wanted to throw something at him. Preferably the glass paperweight with a snow scene in it that held down his papers. Let him laugh *that* off.

"Undoubtedly someone has mistaken your locker for his own. Without a doubt he will discover his mistake and return them to the office tomorrow. I suggest that you check with Mrs. Penner in the morning. Meanwhile we'll put a notice on the bulletin board." He gave her a nod of dismissal.

Annah couldn't believe it. She was surprised he hadn't suggested looking in Lost and Found.

As she got to the door he said, "Oh, and Miss . . . uh . . ."

She turned to look at him.

"Keep your locker locked hereafter. We are here to learn not only our ABC's but our responsibilities, you know." He gave a tight little smile.

So the whole thing is my fault, she thought bitterly. And I'm irresponsible. I hate this stupid school.

She went upstairs again to see if by some miracle the snowshoes had reappeared. The boy named Homer, whose locker was next to hers, came down the hall. "I looked in all the lockers that were open," he said. He looked worried.

"Thanks. That was nice of you."

He blushed. "Your first day at this school, it don't look too good for the school, I guess."

"Well, these things happen." Her mother always said that, and she had always thought it meant absolutely nothing. But one had to say something. This boy looked worried, as if she might be suspecting him. "I guess they'll turn up."

"Sure hope so."

For a moment they stood looking at each other, each waiting for the other to say something. Then Annah closed her locker.

"You want me to show you how to lock it? So's you can get it unlocked again?" He turned the combination, and then showed her how to twirl the numbers and lean on the door at the same time. "They get bent. Y'have to fool with 'em to find out which way. Like mine. Mine's almost off its top hinge. Here, try it." He stood back and she did as he had told her. The door stuck at first, but then it opened with a bang.

"I'm usually around if you have any trouble." He put on his coat and jerked a stocking cap down around his ears and loped off down the hall.

It took Annah a long time to get home. The lake was slippery in some places, and in others there was a layer of crusty snow that her feet broke through. She was chilled and tired and angry when she finally climbed onto the dock. And now she had to tell Aunt Edna that Uncle Joe's snowshoes were gone.

CHAPTER 16

UNT EDNA was trying to be a good sport, but Annah could tell she felt bad about the snowshoes. "Maybe they'll turn up. You use mine."

When Annah left the next morning, Aunt Edna gave her a neatly lettered notice to put on the bulletin board outside the drugstore. LOST: MEN'S SNOW-SHOES, POLAR BRAND. REWARD OFFERED. BOX 26, LOCAL. NO QUESTIONS ASKED.

When Annah got to her locker, three girls went by. One of them said, "Hey, you found your snowshoes."

"No, this is another pair."

One of the girls laughed and said, "What webbed feet you have, Grandmother." They all giggled and walked away.

"Morons," muttered Homer, at his locker.

Aunt Edna's snowshoes were shorter and rounder, and they would not fit all the way into Annah's locker, no matter how hard she pushed. It began to seem as if her whole life was going to be dominated by snowshoe troubles.

"Ask Mrs. Penner if you can leave them in the office," Homer said.

Annah didn't want to ask favors of Mrs. Penner, but she had no choice. Surprisingly, Mrs. Penner agreed. She even gave Annah a slight smile. Maybe, Annah thought, they're afraid I'll sue them.

Mabel Turner, who had not spoken to her before, made a point of asking if she had found her snowshoes.

Her manner was not unfriendly, but Annah thought she detected a gleam in her eyes that meant she was enjoying Annah's difficulties.

Annah tried to forget about the whole business and concentrate on her classes. During lunch, which she ate on the steps again with Dodie, she cut Dodie short when she asked about the snowshoes. "I'm just sick of hearing about them."

Dodie frowned. "It's strange though. There are plenty of kids in this school that I can't stand, but I wouldn't have thought they'd steal stuff." She leaned back against the granite pillar and watched Doris Hay walk off the school grounds with Jamie Fontaine. "That Jamie Fontaine," she said. "He's the handsomest boy in this school."

Annah glanced at her in surprise. She wouldn't have expected shabby, skinny, aloof Dodie to pay attention to boys. Looking at her in that new light, she realized that with the right clothes and something done to her badly cut red-brown hair, Dodie might be quite pretty.

"When I lived with my grandmother," Dodie said dreamily, "I had a friend that looked something like Jamie."

"When did you live with your grandmother?"

"Oh, almost all my life till last year." She paused and looked down. "She died."

"And then you went to live with your parents?"

"*He's* not my parent." She said it with great scorn. "My father died when I was four. He died of the influenza."

"That's awful. I'm sorry."

"It was a long time ago. But I remember him. He

88

was a fireman on the train." She gazed off into space as if she were seeing him. "My gram took me. We had a good time, Gram and me."

"That's good."

"*He* only wants me to do the work. My mother gets drunk, and somebody has to look after the little one, or else they get the Board of Health down on them." She gave an odd little laugh. "So I'm stuck with it. But one of these days . . ." Her eyes were brooding.

Annah studied her new friend's face. She felt as if a different person were talking to her, different from the girl she had had lunch with the day before. People were a lot more complicated than one thought.

"You'd like my Aunt Ed," Annah said. "Maybe you could come over for supper some day?"

"Let me know ahead of time," Dodie said, "so I can fix something for Tommy to eat, in case Mama is drunk."

In case Mama is drunk. The phrase ran through Annah's head off and on during her afternoon classes. In case Mama is drunk. What a terrible "in case" to have to deal with every day, and yet Dodie had said it so casually.

When she was coming out of her last class—English, which she was beginning to decide might be all right— a freshman girl ran up the stairs and called to her, "Annah Perry, Mr. Pierce wants to see you."

Now what, she thought, as she went downstairs. Had she broken some rule without even knowing it?

The principal's door was open, and Annah could see that there was someone else in there, but she couldn't see who it was.

"Go right in," Mrs. Penner said. Her voice was solemn.

Dodie was standing in front of Mr. Pierce's desk, crying. Uncle Joe's snowshoes leaned against the desk.

"You found them!" Annah was so happy to see the snowshoes, it took her a minute to react to Dodie's tears. "What's the matter?"

In a voice like doom Mr. Pierce said, "I regret to say your snowshoes were found in Dodie's locker."

"Dodie!" Annah was so startled, she couldn't make sense of it. Dodie, of all people, wouldn't take her snowshoes. "I don't believe it." As Mr. Pierce began to look huffy, she said, "I mean, there must be some mistake."

Dodie was standing with her face turned away from them.

"We have had a talk," Mr. Pierce said. "You may take your snowshoes with you now." He glanced at Dodie. "I shall have to consider your punishment, Dodie. I will inform you later." He paused. "That will be all." He flapped his hand at them.

By the time Annah had gathered up both pairs of snowshoes, Dodie had already fled. Annah couldn't find her anywhere in the halls. She got her coat and hat and books and went outside. She saw Dodie just disappearing up the street, walking fast and bent forward as if she were ready to run. Annah went after her.

Mabel Turner and a few of her crowd passed Annah. "Hey, I heard Dodie swiped your snowshoes," Mabel yelled at her. The three friends screamed with laughter. "Tell her at least she'll have a nice cozy cell in jail. It beats that pigpen she lives in."

Annah was carrying both pairs of snowshoes over

90

her shoulder. She put them down and grabbed Mabel by the front of her coat.

"Hey!" Mabel tried to pull loose.

"In the first place, I don't believe Dodie did it. In the second place, it's none of your business. In the third place, that's a rotten, miserable, stinking way to talk about anybody."

Mabel looked frightened, but she tried to laugh it off. She glanced back at her friends, who were suddenly quiet. "You let go of me." She struck Annah's hand off her coat. Feeling bolder now that she was free of Annah's grasp, she backed away a few steps and said, "You think you can come in here, causing trouble, where nobody wants you. You just stay out of our business. You're just a summer person, and we hate summer people." She looked at her friends again for support.

One of them said, "Yeah," rather faintly.

"Oh, go to blazes." Annah grabbed her snowshoes and hurried after Dodie, who was out of sight now. She felt shaky with anger. She was pretty sure that somehow Mabel Turner was responsible for the snowshoes disappearing. It would be her idea of a good joke to get Dodie blamed for it.

She followed Dodie's footprints in the snow down a lane. Finally she caught up with her. "Wait up," she called.

Dodie hesitated and then stopped. She was wearing a run-down pair of low shoes, and the ankle-deep snow was soaking her socks. "What do you want?"

"Look at me."

Slowly Dodie lifted her head to look at Annah.

"You didn't take my snowshoes."

Dodie shrugged. "They were in my locker."

"But you didn't take them."

"How do you know? You hardly know me."

"I know you well enough for that."

"All right, I didn't."

"Why did you let Mr. Pierce think you did?"

"I didn't let him. I told him I didn't know anything about it. Why should he believe me? I'm the one that's dirt-poor. I'm the one that's only been in town eight months. I'm the one with the drunk mother and the no-good stepfather who goes to jail for moonshining. It's logical, isn't it?"

"I don't know about logical, but anybody who knows you at all would know it isn't true."

Dodie gave her a long look. "You mean it, don't you? You really do believe me."

"Of course I do."

Dodie's eyes filled with tears. She looked away for a minute. "I don't usually blubber all over the place," she said. She wiped her eyes with her sleeve. "Nobody's been very nice to me since my gram died."

"Well, we're friends, aren't we?" Annah felt a little embarrassed by Dodie's emotion, but she was touched. "Listen, in the morning I'll tell Mr. Pierce he's wrong."

"He won't believe you."

"He'll have to. I bet I know who did it, but I don't have any proof, so I can't say so."

"Me too, I know darned well. But he'll punish me anyway. If he keeps me after school, my stepfather will beat me."

Annah was shocked. "Beat you!"

"Oh, sure." Then, surprisingly, Dodie laughed.

92

"But I can run faster than he can. And I've got a hiding place he doesn't know about. I'll show it to you some day maybe. Thanks for believing me."

Before Annah could answer, Dodie had run off. Annah could see part of the roof of a small house in a hollow with woods behind it. That must be where Dodie lived. She wondered if Dodie would really show her the hiding place.

That night when she wrote one of her long letters to Tillie, she told her all about Dodie, or all that she knew, which she realized was not much. "She's hard to figure out," she wrote. "Not simple souls like you and me, ha ha." She added a postscript: "Do you think Miss Shawn would read a poem of mine if I sent it to her? I don't really know this English teacher. She might laugh at me. Oh, well. Remember our slogan: 'Parting is such sweet sorrow. So long, chum, till it be morrow.' Oodles of love, Annah."

CHAPTER *17*

NNAH had no trouble persuading Mr. Pierce not to punish Dodie. He seemed glad not to have to bother with it.

As the cold weeks went by, Annah began to feel more at home. She got to know the other students and to discover which ones she liked, which she didn't. One she definitely did not like was Mabel Turner, who seemed to have appointed herself Annah's enemy. She had a small following who loyally giggled every time Mabel contradicted or challenged Annah. Most of the teachers ignored it when she did it in class, but Miss Franklin, the English teacher, got tired of it and said so after Mabel had been particularly scornful of a theme Annah had written.

"Mabel," Miss Franklin said, "if you have something constructive to contribute, we would be gratified to hear it, but mockery is not literary criticism."

Those who were Annah's friends smiled and nudged each other, but Mabel sulked.

"Mabel never could write worth a hoot," Dodie said. They were eating lunch in a corner of the home ec room. "So she likes to make fun of other people. I was her target before you came."

"You! You're the best writer in the class."

Dodie blushed and looked pleased. Annah had noticed that since they had become friends, Dodie talked more, not only to her but to other students. Most of

94

them seemed to like her. It wasn't because she was poor, Annah thought, that people hadn't paid much attention to her; it was because she had made herself practically invisible. She didn't do that anymore.

Dodie hadn't mentioned again showing Annah her hiding place, and when Annah walked home with her, they always parted at the turn of the lane. But on that day, at the place where Annah usually turned back, Dodie stopped and said, "The old man's up in the mountains. He won't be back yet awhile, maybe a few days."

"In the mountains? Does he go hunting or what?" It was cold, and Annah couldn't imagine going to the mountains. In early March, the snow up there would still be deep.

Dodie didn't answer the question, but she said, "Come on."

The slush in the road had refrozen in ruts. They passed some pussy willows, and Annah picked some for Aunt Edna.

Finally answering Annah's question, Dodie said, "He works for one of the moonshiners. I'm not supposed to say so, but everybody knows it. There's a bunch of them up behind the Ossipees; they have shooting wars sometimes, and I always hope he'll get shot." She looked at Annah to see if she was shocked.

Annah was, a little, but she could understand. Dodie said things out loud that most people just thought. She changed the subject. "I got a letter from Miss Shawn, that's the English teacher where I used to go. I sent her a poem. She liked it pretty well, but she said I should turn it in to Miss Franklin, because she's my teacher now. Miss Shawn is wonderful. She's read everything."

"Nobody's read everything," Dodie said. "Is that that rich school you went to?"

"It's not really rich." She shouldn't have brought up the subject of her school right after Dodie had told her bad things about her stepfather. It sounded as if she were showing off.

"It costs to go there, doesn't it?" Dodie said.

"Yes, but . . ."

"Then it's for rich kids. Otherwise they'd go to public school like everybody else."

Annah felt criticized, but it was almost funny, Dodie being mad because Annah was "rich," when her family was really down to its last bent nickel, as Herb said. Dodie was prickly sometimes.

They were approaching Dodie's house.

Annah stopped. "I'd better get on home."

"Why? The old man's not around." She grabbed Annah's arm and pulled her along. "You might as well see my hideaway."

Annah was surprised. "All right. I'd like to."

As they came up to Dodie's house, Annah saw that it was a flimsy shack almost ready to fall down. Weeds stuck up through the dirty snow. Some hens were scrabbling at a bare place in the yard. A Chevrolet touring car with a smashed-in fender and a flat tire stood in a patch of snow-covered weeds.

"That's my car," Dodie said. "Gram left it to me, but he keeps saying it's his, 'cause I'm a minor. He got drunk and smashed it up." She turned off on a path leading toward the woods.

There was no one in sight at the house, but as they walked away, Annah heard a small child shout.

Dodie hesitated, looked back, and yelled, "In a minute, Tom." As they walked on, she said, "It's Tommy."

"Who's Tommy?"

"My half-brother."

Annah wanted to ask more questions, but they were walking single file along a trampled path, and it was hard to talk. Besides, she felt shy about asking Dodie personal questions.

Dodie held back a pine bough so it wouldn't hit Annah in the face. "Are you good at keeping secrets?" she asked sternly.

"Sure."

Dodie narrowed her eyes. "Because if you give it away, I'll really be mad."

Annah shivered. It sounded like a threat. "I promise." She felt nervous about being let in on Dodie's secret. What if somebody found out about it, and Dodie blamed Annah? Maybe there was something illegal about Dodie's secret, like her stepfather's moonshining. What if she did take things that weren't hers sometimes, and hid them out here in the woods? You could almost see how she might, when she had been cheated out of what belonged to her. If that man took her car, he probably took everything her grandmother had left her.

"I've got something in here that nobody knows about." Dodie was carefully removing a pile of branches that seemed to be piled against the side of the hill.

She stepped back and Annah exclaimed, "It's a cave!"

"It's a big one," Dodie said proudly. "It goes way back into the hill. I hide out here when I have to get away from them." She got down on her hands and knees. "But that's not the surprise." She thrust her head into the opening. "January . . . January . . . Here, Jannie, Jannie." In a moment she made a scooping motion with her hands and turned around.

Annah drew in her breath and then said, "Ohhh."

In her cupped hands Dodie held a small cottontail rabbit. The peppered brown fur, touched here and there with black, and white on the legs and belly, quivered as Dodie stroked him. He was only about a foot long.

"He's beautiful!" Annah said.

The rabbit's nose wriggled, and his brown ears turned toward her like small antennae picking up on her voice.

"Can I pet him?"

"Yes, but come at him slow. He scares easy."

Very carefully, Annah reached out her fingertips and touched the furry back. The rabbit flicked his ears back and forth. Dodie talked to him softly. His fluffy white tail stood straight up.

"Where'd you get him?" Annah said.

"I found him in a briar patch, just like the stories say. He must have been about two or three weeks old. He was no bigger than my fist, but he had all his fur and he could scamper around and feed himself with grass and stuff."

"Where was his mother?"

"Something must have got her. I never saw her. So I made him a nest in the cave, and I came out and fed him every day till he got bigger."

"Can he get out of the cave?"

"Oh, yeah. He comes and goes. But it's a pretty safe place. Unless a snake or something gets in there.

But Jannie can get out fast." She turned up one of his paws. "Look, they have fur on the bottoms of their feet, like bedroom slippers." She put him down. For a moment he sat very still. Then with a leap he was gone. "He'll be back. You want to see inside the cave?"

A flat, nearly level space near the entrance narrowed as it went further into the hill. It was dark and cold inside, but Dodie had some old half-burned candles and matches, a ragged blanket that looked as if it might have come from the dump, and half a dozen books.

"Sometimes I come out here and read, or just talk to January."

"Why do you call him January?"

"That's when I found him, early in January."

"Then he must be about three months old now. Let's give him a birthday party."

Dodie laughed. "Birthdays are for *years*."

"It's different for rabbits. I'll bring a cake."

Dodie lay down on her back on the dirt floor, looking more relaxed than Annah had ever seen her. "I hope *he* stays away a long time. Maybe there'll be a spring blizzard and he won't be able to get down off the mountain."

"What mountain?" She felt uneasy thinking of the mountains near the lake.

"Oh, up in back of the Ossipees. There's a whole slew of stills up there. Sometimes they have wars among themselves. What the monster does, he acts like their salesman." She laughed. "You think of a salesman, you think of a nice-looking fellow in a three-piece suit and a sample case, smiling and anxious to please, right? That's not exactly how the monster looks."

"How does he look?" Annah was very curious about Dodie's stepfather. In her mind she saw him as eight feet tall with a big black beard and arms like a blacksmith's.

"Well, there's no three-piece suit, no smile, I can tell you that. At least not around home." Dodie sat up and looked intently at Annah. "Why are you being nice to me?"

Annah was taken aback. "I like you."

"Did your aunt tell you to be nice?"

"My aunt? Of course not. She doesn't even know you."

"She didn't say 'be kind to that orphan kid'?"

"You aren't an orphan."

"I might as well be."

"Well, anyway, she didn't. If I could get you to come home with me, you'd see how nice she is. But whenever I ask you, you won't come."

"I don't trust people much."

"You can trust Aunt Ed. She's probably the most trustworthy person I know. Except Margaret."

"Oh, you and your Margaret. You're always talking about Margaret."

Annah never knew what tack to take when Dodie sounded argumentative and touchy.

"I really hate that stuff," Dodie said, "grown-ups thinking they're doing you a big favor to give you a faded dress their kid's outgrown, or to send over a bowl of pudding that their own family's sick of. I've got as many feelings as they have."

Annah risked a joke. "More," she said.

After a moment Dodie grinned. "Do you think I'm strange?"

Annah thought about it. She wanted to be truthful. "Not strange, but different. Interesting." That was the truth. She was certainly not at all like Tillie or Betsy.

"My gram and I used to have contests to see who was the strangest." Dodie smiled as if she were remembering.

"Like what?"

"Well, one time my gram swapped the bedroom upstairs with the living room downstairs. That really didn't count as strange because she had angina and it was hard for her to climb the stairs. What was strange was, she didn't tell anybody. And when the church ladies came for tea, like they did every six months or so when it was her turn, she didn't say a word. They got their cups of tea and their egg salad sandwiches in the dining room, same as always, and then they flocked into what used to be the living room, not even looking 'cause they were chattering the way they did like a flock of chickens. And Mrs. Trueblood sat down like it was the sofa, only it was Gram's bed. And Mr. Flores, the preacher, almost sat down beside her. Had his knees bent and everything. But Mrs. Gaspell let out a shriek, and Mrs. Trueblood nearly fainted. And Gram says, cool as a cucumber, 'Why, my gracious, what are you folks doing making yourselves cozy in my bedroom?'" Dodie's eyes were dancing with amusement.

"That really was strange, all right." Annah tried to imagine her mother or either of her grandmothers doing something like that. Margaret might. She laughed. It *was* funny. "Then did they go upstairs to the living room?"

"Some did. Mrs. Trueblood went home. Oh, my!" Dodie wiped her eyes. "My gram was a card."

"Did people get mad at her?"

"Sure, lots of them did. The good ones just laughed."

After a minute Annah said, "I guess I ought to be going home."

"You don't like my cave."

"It's a dandy cave. But if I don't get home before it starts to get dark, Aunt Edna worries."

Dodie used her thumb and forefinger to extinguish the one candle she had lighted. She bent over so she could get out of the cave. "Your aunt Edna won't approve of me."

"Why not? Sure she will."

"No, I can tell. She won't want you hanging around with an Orphan Annie like me."

"It's not fair to say that. You haven't even met her."

"Oh, I know these women." She cocked her head at the sound of a child's voice screaming. "I've got to go."

Before Annah could think of anything to say, Dodie was running recklessly down the hardly visible path, crashing into branches, her long legs flying out. Then she was gone and the woods were very still.

There was nothing to do but go home. Annah worked her way along, trying not to tear her coat on the trees. Where the path turned, she stopped a moment and looked back. January was sitting in the entrance to his cave, watching her, nose twitching as if he were about to sneeze.

"Bye, January," she said. She wished she had a rabbit.

CHAPTER 18

"'D LOVE to meet Dodie," Aunt Edna said. It was a Saturday morning, and she and Annah had walked through the woods to town to pick up the mail and some groceries. It was still dark and wintry in the woods, but the surface of the lake now was softening. It was easier to walk through the woods than to snowshoe in the slush.

"I want you to. You'd like her, I think. But she's funny about meeting people, especially grown-ups. She thinks they feel sorry for her, and she hates that."

"I don't blame her. Well, I don't know what feelings I might have about her, but pity wouldn't be one of them."

"Sometimes in the middle of the night I wake up and think about Uncle Herb," Annah said. "It seems crazy to throw your life away just because you've lost your money."

"Money, making it, was the only life Herbert had, I guess." She stopped and pointed to a fox whose bright eyes stared at them from behind a clump of bushes. For a moment they looked at each other, and then he turned and went deeper into the woods, as if he had lost interest in them.

When they got back to the cottage, both of them settled down to read their letters. Annah had Margaret's weekly short letter, written carefully. Annah could imagine her, with the little leather-bound dictionary at hand in case she wasn't sure of a spelling. Margaret was proud of her reading and writing ability.

"My dear Annah," she wrote. "It must be spring. Town meeting here last week, and everybody yelling at everybody else as usual. Richie's dad got re-elected to the school committee. Peter's father got on the board of selectmen, but it was close. I got me a raise and a new job, if you call it new. I'm head of baking. Got me one of those tall white caps, like in the adverts. Went by your house yesterday. Thought about spitting on the FOR SALE sign but was afraid I'd get arrested. Saw Tillie on the streetcar. She misses you something fierce. Me too. Yours truly, Margaret the Baker."

Annah pictured the house as Margaret had seen it. In her mind she walked through the empty rooms, her steps echoing.

"What is it?" Aunt Edna had noticed her distress.

"Oh, when I think of our house, empty and for sale, and that stupid FOR SALE sign, it makes it really not our house anymore."

Aunt Edna came over to the couch and sat beside her. She reached for a plate of fudge on the table and gave Annah a piece. "About houses. I know how you feel. Especially the one you've grown up in, or one you've been especially happy in. Joe and I lived in many places, but leaving some of those houses nearly broke my heart. A little cottage in the south of France, where we lived for two years right after we were married . . ." She broke off. "But in time I learned some things. I found out you don't really lose them. That cottage is as vivid to me, even the wine stain on the bedroom floor . . ." She smiled. ". . . as vivid as it was when I was actually there. Memories stay. They're part of us, part of what makes life rich. I can sit here by the fire and think about the times with Joe, the wonderful and often crazy things we did, the places we went, the people we knew and loved. . . ." Her voice broke but she was still smiling. "I'll never lose any of it. It's me."

They were both quiet for a few minutes.

"Thanks for talking to me," Annah said.

Aunt Edna patted her knee and got up. "I know it's hard to believe what adults tell you. We all have to find out these things ourselves." She took a deep breath. "How would you feel about roast beef hash for supper?"

"Great. I think I'll go skate for a little while. The ice is sloppy, but it's still there."

Aunt Edna nodded. "Have a good time."

Annah put the unopened letter from her mother in the pocket of her mackinaw and got her mittens and cap and her skates.

She walked along the edge of the lake, past the closed-up cottages to the far end where the ice was usually swept clean by the wind. The sky was the color of tin, and there was a sharpness in the wind. She thought of January and was glad he had a snug cave. No snakes would bother him at this time of year. They would still be dormant in the cold weather. How odd it must be to sleep away half the year, to wake up half a year older not knowing what had been going on in the world. Maybe that was happening to her. How would it be when spring woke her up? She looked off toward the mountains, especially Mount Tumble-Down-Dick, where Herb and her father liked to fish for brook trout. It looked cold and forbidding in this light.

She sat on a log to put on her skates, then skated

for a long time, in wider and wider circles, ignoring the slushy water that sprayed up around her ankles. She pretended she was a star in the Ice Follies, and her partner was that nice boy at school, Jamie. In her mind she sang a Strauss waltz, and dipped and swirled, and for the moment forgot everything except how pleasant it felt.

Out of breath, she went back to the shore and sat down to rest for a minute. She felt warm, but the sky was darkening and a few snowflakes floated down slowly. Still, she wasn't quite ready to go back to the cottage.

She took her mother's letter out of her pocket. It was a longer one than usual, and the tone was different, more cheerful. She had joined Grandmother's bridge club, and they had taken the train to Miami to shop. Next week they were going out in a boat on the Okefenokee Swamp. "Last night we had dinner at the Boca Club," she wrote, "and I met a man who sells real estate in Palm Beach. According to him, there is no shortage of money there. He says they need some snappy salesmen. Or saleswomen, he added, but he was making a joke of course. I've written your dad about it. He'd be a good salesman. You probably know he's had a temporary job as a janitor for some person who is on vacation. Your father a janitor! Imagine!" She enclosed a postcard from Herb with a picture of the lobby of the new Waldorf Astoria Hotel, and his message: "Herbert W. Perry made a phone call in the lobby of this hotel."

She put the letter away and tried to picture them all doing the things they were doing. It was so odd. They seemed planets away.

She decided to skate along the edge of the lake instead of walking home.

She was glad Herb had stayed in New York. That, at least, was a place she had been to and could imagine. She'd been to Chicago and Florida too, but they seemed much more remote.

She was so busy thinking, she didn't notice at first how hard it was snowing. A spring storm. She was still on skates, and the going was rough, especially now that she couldn't see very well. She moved a little farther out where the visibility was better. The dark mass of the island was not far away, and she didn't want to get too close.

She stubbed the toe of her skate on a patch of hardened snow and wrenched her ankle. The pain made her gasp. It was the left ankle, which she had broken once long ago.

She stood still, waiting for the pain to subside. If only she could sit down for a minute, but the middle of the lake was not an inviting place. She took a tentative step and winced. If she could relace her shoe skate, that would give her some support. She looked again at the island. It was really quite close. She could sit down on a log or something and tighten the laces on her skate. It was silly to be nervous about a perfectly ordinary island. There was nobody around. She certainly didn't believe in ghosts and monsters and all that little kid stuff.

Trying not to think about those silly things, she limped to the shore of the island and sat down on a log. She unlaced her skate and poked gently at her ankle. It didn't seem to be swelling, not yet anyway. She supposed she should get one of those Ace bandage things.

She put the skate on again and laced it more tightly. The wind had come up and was blowing snow in her face, tiny pellets that stung. The tall pines at her back protected her some from that direction. A little way from where she sat was the boathouse, all locked up for winter. She wondered why anyone would want to build a house on an island. In the middle, where the cottage was, you wouldn't be able to see past the trees, they were so dense. Maybe the Sprouls had some terrible secret in their lives, something worse than Crazy Albert, that they liked to hide.

She had been holding her mittens in her teeth while she laced her shoe. They were the nice ones she'd gotten for Christmas, and she didn't want to lose them in the dark. Her fingers were numb with cold, but she managed to finish the lacing and tie the knot.

She stood up, holding onto a scrub oak bush for balance. Suddenly there was a crashing sound right behind her. She yelled and scrambled away from the shore so fast that she nearly fell down. It had to be Crazy Albert and he probably meant to kill her.

CHAPTER 19

ANNAH was halfway to Aunt Edna's cottage before she slowed down. The noise on the island had stopped. Maybe the creature was right behind her, waiting to pounce. She couldn't stand it: She had to look back. She peered into the half-darkness. On the shore where she had been sitting was the humped silhouette and antlers of a moose.

A moose! She felt like a fool. Not that a moose was a creature she would go right up to and say hello, but she certainly didn't think of one as scary, except maybe in mating season. A couple of summers ago, she and her father had come upon one knee-deep in the lake, eating water lilies. He had lifted his head to stare at them with big, dark eyes, a bunch of long-stemmed lilies hanging from his mouth. The sight was so funny, Annah had burst out laughing. That moose had stood there chewing, his long upper lip going up and down as if he was trying to get something out of his tooth. Then he turned on his spindly legs, all fourteen hundred pounds of him, and clopped off into the woods.

Maybe this was the same moose. And she had let herself be terrified without even finding out what she was afraid of. And she had lost her mittens.

During the next few days it snowed so hard that she couldn't go to school. She spent a lot of time working on a theme for English. She was writing about the moose and the island and how stupid it was to be frightened when you didn't even know what it was you were afraid of. She wanted to put something in about Uncle Herb being so frightened that he threw his life away, but she couldn't seem to find a way to connect it with the moose.

While she was shut up in the cottage with Aunt Edna, she began to notice in little ways that Herb had been right about Aunt Edna's grieving for Uncle Joe. A couple of times she could tell Aunt Edna had been crying, and once when they were playing "An American in Paris" on the wind-up phonograph, Aunt Edna left the room quickly. That music had been in a musical called *Show Girl* that was the last New York show Aunt Ed and Uncle Joe had seen together.

Annah tried to find ways to cheer her up. She found two packs of cards and got her to play double solitaire. They had some wild games, and Annah was glad to hear Aunt Edna laughing again.

They made popcorn and brownies and planned elaborate meals, some of which never got cooked. The snow on the windowsills reached halfway to the top of the windows, and the wind howled in the chimney. Sometimes Henry howled back.

Aunt Ed taught Annah to hold a kernel of popcorn above her head at arm's length and drop it accurately into her mouth. She also taught her to play mumblety-peg. They went through nearly all of Aunt Ed's large collection of phonograph records.

On the last day of the storm Annah put on her boots and coat and cap and her old mittens to take Henry for a walk. She had never told Aunt Ed what happened to her Christmas mittens.

Outside, she shoveled the snow off the millstone at the back door and tramped through the knee-deep snow with Henry picking his way in her footprints. She climbed up to the top of the boulder and tried to see the lake, but the thick curtain of snow cut everything off.

Henry saw a squirrel and chased it, forgetting that he hated deep snow. He floundered like a small ship.

When Annah came into the sun porch, stamping the snow from her boots, Aunt Edna said, "The *Herald* says they're boating on the Charles. Spring, in case you hadn't noticed, has sprung."

That night Annah woke to the sound of rain, and by morning the woods were clothed in a thin shimmering coat of ice and the skies had cleared.

The next morning Annah thought of January's birthday cake. "Aunt Ed, can I have half of that cake you made yesterday?" She grinned. "It's for a birthday. A rabbit's."

Aunt Edna laughed. "Happy to do my bit. Any rabbit we know?"

"Dodie's little cottontail. January."

"I wish I had some candles. And a big candy J."

Aunt Edna cut off half of a chocolate cake, and while Annah was eating breakfast, she frosted it and packed it carefully in waxed paper and then in a paper bag.

"Carry it right side up if you can."

By the time Annah got to school, she had managed not to fall down on the slippery surface of the lake and not to turn the cake upside down.

She was placing it carefully on the floor of her

locker when Dodie came along. "I brought the cake," she said.

"What cake?" Dodie looked somber, and there was a bruise on her forehead.

"For you-know-who's birthday."

"Oh, yeah. I forgot. That's great." Dodie's face lit up.

"Whose birthday?" It was Mabel Turner, standing behind them with three of her friends.

Annah could have kicked herself for not making sure she and Dodie were alone before she mentioned the cake. "Oh, it's just a joke, Mabel," she said. She stood in front of the locker, hoping to block the sight of the cake.

Mabel peered over her shoulder. "Is that it? Whose party? How come you didn't ask us? I don't think that's very friendly. Do you kids think that's friendly?" she asked her friends.

"No," they chorused dutifully. "We don't think it's friendly at all."

"Move, Mabel, will you?" Annah said. "I'm trying to close my locker." She had given up locking it; it was too much trouble.

Mabel made an elaborate step backward. "Oh, certainly, we'll move. We know when we're not wanted. If outsiders want to stay outsiders, that's their tough luck. Come on, girls." She swept down the hall with her allies behind her.

"Me and my big mouth," Annah said.

"Never mind. She'll forget it. Listen, let's go out to the you-know-where right after school, and have the you-know-what. What kind is it?"

"Chocolate, with mocha frosting."

"Wild!" Dodie clutched her stomach. "And best of all, the old man's away again."

All day Annah looked forward to January's party. She could hardly wait to write Richie about the birthday party for a rabbit. He'd get a kick out of that.

She carried the bag with the cake very carefully as they walked up the road to Dodie's house. Dodie's mother was hanging out clothes in the yard, with a small child sitting in the snow beside her.

"Wait a sec." Dodie ran up to them, scooped up the child and took him inside the house, and then took the clothespins from her mother and hung up the clothes. Her mother watched for a minute, her arms folded over her chest as if she were cold. Then she went inside. She was a small, thin woman with straggly hair and a look of defeat.

"How many children are there?" Annah asked. It was amazing how little she really knew about Dodie's home life. When Dodie didn't answer, she felt embarrassed about having asked. "I just wondered. You never talk about them."

"There's one," Dodie said. "A boy. Now you know my family history, just like the Board of Health, the school authorities, and all those big wheels."

Annah flushed. "I'm sorry. I didn't mean to be nosy."

"Ah, it's all right. I'm touchy. I've had to put up with too many people asking too many questions. People can't believe a person can look out for her own folks." Then in a different voice she said, "Let's stick a little pine cone in the cake for a candle. I hope Jannie's there."

The snow was melting, and it took a while to slog through the deep, wet snow to the cave. Dodie looked for tracks, but they were hard to find in that kind of snow. "Those little furry slippers of his don't leave much trace anyway." She pulled away the snow-covered brush in front of the cave.

Annah sat on a rock. "Shall I open the cake?"

"Yeah." Dodie stuck her head in the cave, calling January. After a minute his face appeared, nose twitching furiously. He hopped outside and moved to the protection of a bush to watch them.

"If there's any cake left," Annah said, "why don't you take it home to your little brother?" Then quickly added, "If you want to. I don't mean to butt in."

Dodie laughed and tossed a handful of snow at her. "Of course I want to. It's a good idea." She took off her wool gloves with the holes in them and rubbed her hands together. "Boy, do I hate to hang out clothes on a cold day! A person could freeze to the clothesline and just hang there."

Carefully, Annah opened up the thick paper bag and took out the waxed-paper package. She frowned, puzzled. "It looks flattened out. How did it . . . I was so careful with it."

"Maybe the cold made it fall a little."

Annah unfolded the waxed paper and gave a cry of dismay. "Look! It got smashed!"

The cake was nothing but a heap of crumbs. It had been throughly battered and then the crumbs heaped together more or less in the form of the original cake. The frosting had been mostly scraped off.

Annah and Dodie stared at each other.

Finally Annah said, "It was a beautiful cake. This couldn't have happened even if I hadn't been careful with it, but I was. Somebody did this."

"Three guesses who," Dodie said bitterly. "Start looking for smears of frosting on a girl with the initials M T."

"She wouldn't, would she?"

"Somebody did. Who else can you think of? She overheard what you said, and she thought we were having a party that she wasn't invited to. Mabel Turner can't stand to be left out." She picked up a handful of crumbs. "They're delicious crumbs." She grinned at Annah. "Cheer up. It's still a great party. I'll take some crumbs home to Tommy. By the time he gets through with a piece of cake, that's what it looks like anyway."

They went into the cave and sat on the blanket. Dodie lit a candle, and they sang "Happy Birthday, dear January," though he stayed outside, watching them.

"Listen," Annah said, "as long as your . . . that man is away, why don't you ask your mother if you can spend the night with us."

"Spend the *night*?" Dodie looked wary. "What would your aunt say?"

"She's been telling me to bring you home."

"Overnight? I don't have a clean nightgown."

"I'll lend you one."

Dodie sat very still for a minute. Then she straightened up. "Why not? Gram always said, 'Take risks. Live it up.'" She made one of those lightning changes in mood that always took Annah by surprise. She gathered up the crumbs, blew out the candle, and eased herself outside the cave. "January, take care of things while I'm gone."

"I'll bring a carrot next time, Jannie," Annah said. "I promise."

"I haven't been away overnight since Gram died,"

Dodie said. "Except the times I ran away." She leaped over a snowbank. "Race you to the road."

Carrying the bag of cake crumbs, Annah followed. Maybe January's birthday party would turn out well after all, in spite of Mabel Turner.

CHAPTER 20

HEN ANNAH stopped at the post office on her way home with Dodie, the postmistress, Charlotte Hunter, who was a friend of Aunt Edna's, said, "Annah, you hit the jackpot!"

Dodie's eyes widened as she saw letter after letter handed out through the window to Annah. A letter from each parent, one from Margaret, one from Tillie, one from Richie, even a short one from Peter. "You must have friends by the millions." Dodie looked wistful.

"Oh, and here's a beat-up postcard from your big brother." One of Mrs. Hunter's famous traits was that she read all the postcards and told the recipients what they said. "He's still in New York, sleeping at the YMCA."

She reached down below the shelf and came up with a flat package, about two by three feet. "This one came Railway Express, but George was shutting up for the day, so he brought it over here." She lifted it up and looked at it. "Says it's from Richard Ebsen."

"Richie!" Annah said. "And it's not even my birthday."

"Maybe it's for January," Dodie said, giggling. She stared at all of Annah's mail. "Do you get this much every day?"

"No." Annah felt bad, because Dodie probably didn't get any mail.

"She gets a slew of it though," Mrs. Hunter said.

"Well, me, I don't believe in writing letters," Dodie said, in her sharp voice that plainly said "Don't feel sorry for me." "Here today and gone tomorrow, that's my slogan."

They walked home through the dripping woods, playing at trying to pull down soaking branches to dump the water on each other. But as they came closer to the cottage, Dodie grew quieter. It occurred to Annah that she was nervous.

"My aunt Ed has heard so much about you, she feels as if she knows you already," Annah said. "You'll like her."

"She won't like me," Dodie said. "I'm a mess. I should have taken a bath. I didn't even comb my hair."

"She's not like that," Annah said.

Aunt Edna saw them coming and walked out to meet them. Before Annah could say anything, she said, "You must be Dodie."

"You can tell by my mink coat," Dodie said.

Annah groaned inwardly. Dodie was going to take that tack: sarcastic, defensive.

But Aunt Edna only laughed, glanced down at her own wool ski jacket and said, "It matches mine. We must shop in the same salon. Bonwit Teller?"

Dodie gave a loud laugh. "You said it."

By the time Aunt Edna had taken them inside for hot chocolate and the other half of January's chocolate cake, Annah had stopped worrying about how Dodie and Aunt Ed were going to get along.

They told her about the disaster with January's cake, but Annah left out their suspicion that Mabel had done it.

"Poor January," Aunt Edna said. "Why don't you take him a jar of my beet greens?"

"He'd love that," Dodie said. "I promised him lettuce, but he knew I was lying. I'd have to go down to Florida or someplace to get lettuce at this time of year."

Florida reminded Annah of her mail, and while she read her letters, Dodie and Aunt Edna began scrubbing baking potatoes and peeling carrots for supper. Annah read her mail quickly, but she saved Richie's package for later until she could open it by herself.

Aunt Edna put a Strauss waltz on the Victrola, and Dodie was waltzing around the kitchen as she peeled carrots. Henry followed her, picking up an occasional piece of carrot, chewing on it experimentally, and spitting it out.

Aunt Edna lined up lamb chops in a pan. "What news from the family?"

"Mother went to Palm Beach to talk to some man about selling real estate. Dad is selling insurance on a commission. Herb is sleeping at the Y or wherever he can, eating at soup kitchens or the Automat, stuffing envelopes for the National Students Federation of America for no pay."

"What's that?" Dodie asked.

"A group that gets anti-fascists out of Europe before they get killed. They try to find them jobs over here."

"That must be a bit difficult," Aunt Edna said, "when our own people can't find jobs."

"Mostly they're scientists and writers and things."

"Annah, dear, set the table, will you?" Aunt Edna said.

During supper, Dodie was so enthusiastic about

the homemade blueberry jam that Aunt Edna got a jar from the cupboard and gave it to her.

Dodie's eyes widened. "Are you giving me that? Listen, I wasn't hinting. I mean . . ."

Aunt Edna interrupted. "I know you weren't. I'd like you to have it. It would be a favor. I did up so much last summer, it's not going to be gone before the blueberries are ripe again."

Dodie hugged the jar to her chest. "Oh, boy! Listen, when they're ripe, I know where all the best highbush berries are. I'll pick you gallons."

"It's a deal," Aunt Edna said. "I hate to pick them. I eat more than I bring home."

Dodie held the jar up to the lamplight. "Tommy is going to love some of this." Then suddenly embarrassed, as if she had said something she didn't intend to say, she added, "He's my half-brother."

"I'll give you another jar for Tommy. That one's for you."

"You'll think I'm a beggar."

"That's the last thing I'd think." She touched Dodie's wrist lightly.

The girls did the dishes and cleaned up the kitchen and Aunt Edna kept the Victrola going. Annah thought of dancing school.

Annah had never seen Dodie in such high spirits. Her eyes sparkled and there was color in her face. At one point during a third playing of "Tales from the Vienna Woods," she pulled Aunt Edna to her feet and danced her wildly around the room. Laughing and amazed, Annah watched them. Not only Dodie, but Aunt Edna too, looked exhilarated. Some of her hairpins had flown out, and her hair curling around her face made her look young, the way she used to look when Uncle Joe was alive. As if life were fun, Annah thought. I ought to be like Dodie, so Aunt Ed would have a better time.

After they had gone to bed at last, Annah and Dodie lay awake a long time, talking.

"As soon as I can get a job and save up some money," Dodie said, "I'm going to get the car fixed. Then I'll just get in and drive away."

"Drive away where?"

"How do I know? Wherever the mood strikes me. Somewhere warm, where it doesn't snow. California, maybe, or Alabama."

"Florida?"

"No, you have to be rich to live in Florida."

Annah gave a sad little laugh. "No, you don't."

"Well, richer than me."

"Do you know how to drive?"

"Sure. Gram taught me. Sort of. I wasn't tall enough to reach the pedals, but I sat in Gram's lap and steered. Do you know how to drive?"

"Yes."

"Then you can help me brush up."

The light from the stove downstairs flickered through a knothole in the floor. They heard Aunt Edna let Henry out, and then call him in. Alice came upstairs and curled up between Annah and Dodie.

"My gram had a cat," Dodie said sleepily. "Tortoiseshell, named Petunia. A tortoiseshell cat is good luck. That's why I thought Gram wouldn't die." She yawned. "But she did." She turned over, and in a few minutes she was breathing regularly.

Annah waited until she was sure Dodie was asleep.

Then she got up quietly and found her flashlight on the table. Picking up Richie's package, she carried it over to a half-walled-off nook where tools and boat supplies were stored. Here she could turn on her light without waking Dodie. Silently she unwrapped the package. Richie had sent her a present twice before, for no particular reason: One was a tiny carved piece of scrimshaw that he had found at an auction; the other was a box of her favorite chocolate-covered orange peels.

It felt like a picture. Her fingers traced the outline of what seemed to be a frame. Maybe it would be one of his own; he painted very well.

She slipped it out of the inner wrapping and turned the light on it. For several minutes she sat absolutely still. It was a watercolor of Annah's house. It had been done with great care, down to the last detail. And it looked lived-in. He had painted in the draperies in the windows as if they were still there. A bicycle, probably his own, leaned against the steps. The hammock was up on the veranda. There were the mugho pines, and the lilacs in bloom. On the third floor, the dormer window in Herb's room was open, as if he were about to stick his head out and yell hi, and part of the white curtain was blowing out.

The bay window on the dining room side was a little bit out of proportion, and the first floor windows were not quite tall enough, but the effect was so real, and it moved Annah so deeply, that she literally couldn't move for several minutes. Silent tears streamed down her face.

She jumped as she felt a touch on her shoulder.

"What are you looking at?" Dodie whispered.

Annah held it up. "Richie did a watercolor of my house." She wiped the tears away. "It made me homesick."

Dodie took it and looked at it a long time. "It's a beautiful house."

"It is to me."

"It looks like a palace."

"Oh, Dodie. It's just a house. It's because I grew up in it that I love it so much."

Annah put the picture carefully on the bureau. When they were in bed again, Dodie said, "You were crying."

"Oh, it just took me by surprise."

After a minute Dodie said, "My gram had a nice house, but it was about a fourth as big as yours."

"Well, we had more people. There were just the two of you." She felt closer to Dodie than she ever had before. Maybe because of the picture, and because it was dark. They could talk without looking at each other. "Tell me about your gram's house."

"Oh, it was what they call a Cape Cod, although Cape Cod is a long way off. Real small. I'll draw you a picture sometime. Not a good one, like Richie's. He's a real artist, isn't he."

"Yes, he is." And a real friend, Annah added in her mind. She stayed awake long after Dodie had gone back to sleep.

CHAPTER 21

*T*HE DAY the spring issue of the school literary magazine came out, Dodie was not in school. Annah hadn't even known that Dodie had submitted a story. It was too bad she wasn't there, because the story made quite a stir. It was a funny, wild tale about an inexperienced and timid revenue officer who was trying to track a particular moonshiner back in the mountains. But the moonshiner, who had sampled an especially deadly batch of his own product, got his identity confused, and he tracked the revenue officer. By the time they caught up with each other, they were both so mixed up and so frightened by a mountain lion, they embraced each other like old friends and went back to the moonshiner's place to get happily drunk.

Mabel, of course, was critical. "All that mixup about who's who, and getting drunk and all, I don't think that's funny," she said, after Miss Franklin had read the story to the class.

"Shakespeare found it amusing," Miss Franklin said.

"What?" Mabel looked blank.

One of her friends poked her in the ribs and said, "Mistaken identity. Getting drunk and all bolluxed up."

Miss Franklin smiled. "That's it, Bertha."

Bertha smiled smugly.

"I like Dodie's story," Miss Franklin said. "It has a crazy, far-out irony." She looked over her glasses, amused. "And if you want a moral, there it is: Stay away from moonshine. It addles your brains."

"Dodie ought to know." Mabel's words were just audible. Miss Franklin drew in her breath as if to protest, and then decided to ignore it.

Annah was glad Dodie wasn't there to hear Mabel's last remark, but she wished she had heard the rest. Her own effort, a poem, was on one of the last pages. When she read it now, she wondered why she, or anyone, had liked it. It wasn't nearly as original as Dodie's story. She decided to take a copy of the magazine to Dodie right after school.

She could hardly wait for school to end. Maybe Dodie had had to stay home with Tommy. Sometimes she did when her mother got too drunk to look after him.

As soon as school was out, she headed up the road toward Dodie's. She had never actually gone into the house.

She stopped short when she got to Dodie's yard. Someone was pounding, a harsh sound of metal on metal. The noise stopped, and a tall burly man in a wool plaid shirt stood up, holding a big hammer in his hand. He had been trying to hammer the badly bent fender away from the wheel.

Annah was too startled to say anything. He must be "the man," Dodie's stepfather. He had big shoulders like a blacksmith, and long stringy black hair. There were streaks of dirt on his face.

He stared at Annah and finally said, "Who are you?"

Dodie's mother came out of the house carrying

the little boy. He looked too big to be carried, but she didn't get a good look at him because his mother turned around at once and went back into the house.

"I was looking for Dodie," Annah said.

"Well, she ain't here. If you see her, you tell her to git on home, or she'll wish she had."

He began banging on the fender again.

Annah walked away. She was halfway out to the road when she thought of the cave. She made a long detour so that the man in the yard wouldn't see her.

At first she thought there was no one in the cave, but when her eyes got used to the light, she saw Dodie huddled in her blanket, staring at the ground.

"Dodie! Are you all right?"

Dodie looked up slowly. There was a bruise under Dodie's left eye and a cut on her jaw. "Hi," she said.

"What happened?"

"I stayed out here all night."

"It's too cold."

"January kept me company."

"Why'd you stay out here?"

"We had a fight about the car. I've got the old registration. He tried to get it away from me." She patted her pocket with a tight little smile. "Ha ha. I've still got it."

"Why does he want it?"

"He's trying to say Gram sold the car to him. He thinks if he has the old registration, they'll believe him." A fit of shivering shook her and she pulled the blanket closer around her.

"Listen, come home with me for the weekend. You'll get sick if you stay out here. Come on, Dode." She pulled her to her feet.

"Tommy—"

"He'll be all right. I just saw him. Your mother looked all right."

"You saw my brother? Tommy?"

"Just for a sec. She carried him inside as soon as she saw me."

Dodie gave her a searching look. "Well, all right."

Annah took off her coat and handed it to Dodie. "I don't need it. I practically ran up here from school, and I'm all heated up. I wanted to show you the magazine."

She showed it to Dodie and told her about the praise Miss Franklin had given it.

"Shakespeare?" Dodie laughed hoarsely. "Must have been Miss Franklin's day to crack jokes."

"It's the first story in the magazine. That means it's the best."

"Means it's the longest." But Dodie was pleased. She kept looking at the magazine as they followed the long muddy road around the lake, since it was no longer safe to walk on the ice.

Annah glanced sideways at her face. "He hit you, didn't he."

"Only because he took me by surprise. We were arguing about Tommy. He didn't hit me again, not after I went after him with the butcher knife."

"Dodie! You didn't!"

"I did. He said he was going to get the cops on me. Ha ha ha. The day he goes near a cop when he doesn't have to, ice cream'll freeze in hell." Dodie was shivering in spite of the warm coat, and her teeth chattered when she talked.

Annah was relieved when they finally came in sight of the cottage. Aunt Edna was outside, painting a watercolor of three pitch pines that hung over the edge of the lake. She didn't act surprised to see Dodie. "Hello, you two. I've just taken up watercolor. What do you think?" She looked more closely at Dodie. "You look ill."

"I think she's caught a cold."

"Come inside and have a hot bath. There's plenty of hot water for once. I was going to do the laundry and trying to find excuses not to."

"Now you have one." Dodie grinned at her.

Aunt Edna built up the fire in the stove, and got her own warm flannel robe for Dodie. "Annah, honey, fill up the two hot water bottles, will you? I'll heat up some of that soup we had last night."

Later, when she was bundled up on the sofa by the Franklin stove, eating chicken soup, Dodie said to Aunt Edna, "You'd make a great mother." She sounded hoarse, but she was no longer shaking.

Annah thought for a moment that Aunt Edna looked sad when Dodie said that, but perhaps she had imagined it. Annah's mother thought that every woman who didn't have children must be languishing away with a broken heart, but Annah wondered if it was necessarily so.

"Speaking of mothers," Aunt Edna said, "we'd better get word to your mother. She'll be worrying about you."

Dodie sighed and closed her eyes. "I doubt that. Unless there's work to be done. Anyway, I guess it can wait till morning." She opened her eyes and gave Aunt

Edna a rueful grin. "My mother is not known as a great worrier."

Later in the evening, when Dodie had fallen asleep on the sofa, Aunt Edna and Annah sat in the kitchen with the door closed, Annah translating Caesar and Aunt Edna reading the day-late *Boston Transcript*.

There was a knock on the sun porch door. Annah got up to answer it, and found Mabel Turner's grandparents with some fresh-caught bass. An eddy of cool night air rushed into the kitchen with them.

"What you sitting out here for?" Mr. Turner said. "When you going to get that stove fixed, Ed? She smokes like a politician."

He quieted his voice as Aunt Edna explained about Dodie's being asleep in the other room.

"I'm glad you and she are friends, Annah," Mabel's grandmother said. "She can use a good friend. I knew her grandmother. A mite eccentric, but a heart good as gold."

"I hope her family isn't worried about where she is," Aunt Edna said.

"Pah!" Joe Turner said. "A fat lot they care. We ought to figure some way for her to get out of there."

"I'll ask Harry LeBlanc to tell them she's here now," Mrs. Turner said. "That way, that crazy stepfather won't bother you."

Annah felt relieved. She had been picturing that wild stepfather bursting in on them. Chief LeBlanc was the town's one policeman, and although he was one of the kindest, gentlest men in town, he could be tough if necessary.

A short time later, Annah excused herself and went

upstairs to finish her homework. She stopped to look at Dodie, still asleep, her face flushed. Annah looked down at her, thinking how different people looked when they were asleep, with all their defenses down. In a way, it wasn't fair to look at them. She gathered up Alice and went upstairs.

CHAPTER 22

IN THE MORNING, Dodie still had a fever and a bad cough and sore throat. Although Annah felt very sorry for her the first few days, by the end of the week when Dodie began to feel better, she was almost envious. Dodie and Aunt Edna seemed to be having such a good time together.

They played Chinese checkers and Parcheesi and double solitaire, ate lots of food between meals, "both the nourishing and the sinful kinds," Aunt Edna said, and confided in each other more than either of them ever had to Annah. Or so it seemed to her. She had not known, for instance, that Dodie's grandmother had left her house to Dodie, but soon after she died, it burned to the ground.

"You never told me that," Annah said.

"They thought it was set, but they couldn't prove it," Dodie said. "*I* know who set it on fire. It was him. He was mad when he found out Gram left the house to me. He thought he and my mother should have it."

"But you *don't know* he did it," Aunt Edna said gently.

"I know well enough. Nobody else would do it. Same as the car. He'll wreck it before he'll let me have it."

Dodie was beginning to look upset, and Annah could tell that Aunt Edna wanted to distract her. "It's such a lovely warm day," she said, "and most of the ice is gone from the lake. If you two would like to take the rowboat along the shore a way, we could get it out."

Both girls were excited by that idea. The three rolled the old boat out from under the house on the wheeled platform Uncle Joe had made for it, and maneuvered it down to the cove. When it was finally in position to slide into the water, Dodie grabbed a big pine cone and hit the boat on the bow. "I christen thee U.S.S. Aunt Edna!"

With a splash that sent cold water high into the air, the flat-bottomed boat slid into the cove and bobbed on its own wake.

"Stay close to shore," Aunt Edna said, "and keep an eye out for floating chunks of ice. They're not all gone yet." She found one more warm sweater for Dodie while Annah fitted the oarlocks and got the oars from under the house.

Except for that magic feeling in the air, it wasn't as easy to see signs of spring up here in the land of evergreens and water as it was at home, Annah thought. But a minute later Dodie pointed out a high V of Canada geese overhead.

"Pretty soon the loons will be nesting," she said. "One year up to the lake near Gram's I found a nest. I used to hide in the rushes down by the shore and watch after they got big enough to see."

"Oh, I love loons. I love that wild screamy laugh. My brother used to hide his head under his pillow so he couldn't hear it. And I love the way they take off across the water like a seaplane."

"I never saw a seaplane," Dodie said. She gazed

across the water. "When I get my motor car to running, I'm going to travel everywhere and see everything."

"I thought you said it wouldn't run."

"I'm going to ask Homer. He knows about cars. If he'll fix it for me, I'll help him do his algebra."

"What about your . . . about Mr . . ." Annah never knew how to refer to Dodie's stepfather.

"Oh, we'll do it when he's gone."

"But you can't drive."

"You're going to teach me. You and Homer."

To Annah, the idea of getting Dodie's smashed car to run, teaching her to drive, and waving good-bye to her as she drove off to see the world seemed about as unlikely as rowing the old rowboat over to England.

She pushed a bailing can toward Dodie with her foot. "Bail out some of that water near your feet, will you? The old tub needs to be caulked and scraped. Uncle Joe used to do it every year, if they were here."

Dodie began to bail. "I know. Aunt Edna told me. When he got started, he gave every single blessed thing a fresh coat of paint. She said he'd have painted the dog if he could have got him to stand still." She laughed. "They must have had themselves a time."

"She never tells me stuff like that," Annah said.

Dodie glanced up at her. "Well, you needn't be jealous. It's just a whole lot easier to tell things to people you aren't that close to. I know all about that."

Annah looked over her shoulder to get her bearings. She was staying close to shore, but she didn't want to run aground. They were not far from the island now. It still looked dark, but not as forbidding as it had when the snow was on it.

"I lost my new mittens over there by the island," she said, "one day when I was skating."

"Well, let's go find 'em. Now the snow's gone, they'll show up. Do you mean those pretty red ones?"

"Oh, we'd never find them now." She was sorry she had mentioned it.

"How'd you lose them?"

Annah grinned. "A moose startled me and I dropped them. I thought it was that boy . . ."

Dodie interrupted her excitedly. "Do you know Albert? He's one of my buddies."

Annah looked at her blankly. "Buddies? Albert Sproul?"

"Sure. I love Albert. I got to know him last summer. I was walking along the shore, right about over there by that little cove, and I heard this fantastic music. So I swam over to the island, because that's where it was coming from."

"What was it?"

"Albert. He was playing Mozart. Anyway, he said it was Mozart, and it sounded great to me."

"We must be talking about different people."

"No, no, Albert Sproul. People in town call him Crazy Albert, but they're just ignorant."

"You mean he was playing records?"

"Of course not. His piano. Didn't you ever hear him play?"

"I've never even . . ." Annah interrupted herself. "No, I didn't know he played anything. How could he? I mean he's . . ."

"Crazy? Don't you believe it. Part of him in his head didn't grow up, that's all. But the music part of him is wonderful. Hey, maybe they're here. They said they come up some weekends in spring. Aim the boat that way, why don't you?"

Annah was scared. She couldn't make sense out of what Dodie had just told her. Maybe Dodie was crazy, too. "Aunt Edna said for us not to leave the shoreline," she said.

"Oh, come on. Except for a couple of sink holes, there's no place deeper than eight feet between here and the island. You can walk most of it. Please, Annah. I'd love to see Albie. He hasn't been up for ages. His mother is in bad health, but sometimes he and his dad come. They're great pals. Come on, we won't stay long."

Against her better judgment, Annah pulled on one oar to turn the boat toward the island. How could a crazy person like Albert play the piano? Maybe it was one of Dodie's jokes. She prayed that the Sprouls were not on the island this weekend.

But a minute later Dodie bounced in her seat and said, "Oh, good! There's a light!"

"Sit still!" Annah said, more crossly than she meant to. "You'll swamp us." She sounded fierce because she was scared. "We'd better go home."

"No! Oh, Annah, please! If you don't dock at the island, I'll jump out and wade ashore. And probably get pneumonia," she added darkly.

"I don't see any dock."

"Around to your left. Starboard or port or whatever it is."

Annah knew perfectly well where the dock was. She just didn't want to land. But a moment later the bow scraped the edge of the dock next to an outboard with the name ALBIE painted on the bow.

She was about to suggest that she would wait in

the boat while Dodie went to pay her visit, but Dodie was already hallooing, cupping her hands and yelling loud enough to wake the bears in their dens.

"Hallo, hallo! Is anybody home? Albie? It's me, Dodie."

For a blessed few minutes Annah thought no one was there. Then she heard a whoop, and the familiar crashing sound. She wished it were only the moose, but a moose doesn't yell, "Hello!" in a bass voice. She took a firm hold on one of the oars.

Dodie was already out of the boat, running up the path, as Albert emerged. It was the first time Annah had had a real look at him. He was not quite as big as she had thought, but he was a tall, stout boy with a big head and a mop of dark hair that fell almost to his eyes. He had a strange, unsteady walk, like drunken sailors in the movies. She could see why he made so much noise as he walked through the woods; he tramped right through bushes, and sometimes crashed into trees without seeming to notice. He kept his hands stretched out in front of him, moving his arms a lot.

His face was broad, and just now he was grinning and chuckling. There was something odd about his eyes.

"Dodie?"

She was running toward him, and he seemed to be looking past her. All at once Annah realized he had trouble seeing. As Dodie got close to him, he seemed to focus on her face, squinting his eyes. He jumped up and down like a child.

"Dod . . . eee!"

"Albie, old buddy, how ya been?" Dodie threw her long arms around him and gave him a hug.

136

Clumsily he hugged her back.

"I'm so glad to see you. How's everything going? How's your mother?" Dodie was talking fast.

"Good, good, good. She's at . . . uh . . ." He fumbled for the word. "Mount Clemens. In the spa. They got health baths. You want to come see Pop?"

"Sure I do, and I want to hear you play." As if she had just remembered Annah, she said, "I've got a friend I want you to meet." She beckoned to Annah. "She lives over on the point. You'll like her."

Annah was still clutching the oar. She saw Albert pull back a little, and saw his expression change. He's afraid of me, she thought. I'm afraid of him, he's afraid of me. She put down the oar and got out of the boat. When she got close to him, he looked bigger than before. "Hello, Albert," she said. "I'm Annah."

He pulled his hands back and tucked them inside his sleeves like a child. She was amazed that she could have been afraid of him.

"Dodie says you play the piano," she said.

He didn't answer. Instead, he looked worried.

Dodie put her hand on his arm. "It's all right, Albie. Annah's a friend. You remember her uncle, Mr. Joe Driskill."

His face brightened. "Mr. Joe! Yeah, we were friends. He took me fishing." Then he looked sad. "Mr. Joe got killed."

"Yes, he did," Annah said. "I live with his wife now. She's my aunt. Aunt Edna."

"Mrs. Edna. I know Mrs. Edna. Nice lady."

So suddenly that Annah was startled, he stuck out his big hand. "How ya do."

"How do you do, Albert. I'm glad to meet you."

"Albie, will you play for us?" Dodie said.

"Yeah, sure. Pop will get us some sarsaparilla. You like sarsaparilla? We got Moxie too." Clumsily he turned around and lumbered up the path to the cottage, which was set back in a grove of trees. The cottage itself was dark green, which made it hard to see from any distance. Smoke was coming out of the chimney, and there was a lamp lighted inside.

A man came out onto the porch. In contrast to his son, he was a small wisp of a man, the kind of man, Annah thought, that you expected to see riding as a jockey, tiny but muscular. His narrow face lit up when he saw Dodie.

When they had greeted each other and Annah had been introduced, he invited them inside. The big living room was comfortably furnished with rustic furniture and, dominating everything, a baby grand piano.

"How did you ever get the piano to the island?" Annah said.

"Rafted 'er," Mr. Sproul said proudly. "I got hold of Billy Fraser, and he got a bunch of his pals, and they put together a raft with some oil drums to float 'er. Brought 'er over here pretty as a picture."

"I'd like to have seen that," Annah said.

"It was a sight. My wife nearly had a conniption, she was so scared the whole thing was going to tip over. But I got great faith in Billy Fraser."

"Oh, me too," Annah said.

He asked after Aunt Edna, and mentioned his sadness at Uncle Joe's death. "They're about the only folks we really knew up here, other than Billy."

"People are scared of me," Albert said. He sounded so forlorn, Annah felt a sharp pain of remorse at her own stupidity.

"It's just because you're such a big boy, Albie," his father said soothingly. "Sometimes you startle 'em a little, but that's just 'cause they don't know you."

"You don't scare me any, Albie boy," Dodie said. "How about playing for us? Annah's dying to hear you."

Albert looked shy.

"I'd love to hear you," Annah said. In spite of what Dodie had said about Mozart, she expected some simple tune, even "I love coffee, I love tea."

"I'll play if you won't look at me," Albert said. "Promise you won't look."

"We'll sit over by the fireplace," his father said, "and I'll bring the girls some sarsaparilla."

"They might like Moxie or birch beer better," Albert said.

Mr. Sproul laughed. "They might, Albie, but all we've got is sarsaparilla." He went out into the kitchen.

Dodie and Annah sat together on a small wicker sofa, facing the woods. Annah was surprised to find that she could see the lake from here. It was quite a nice, cozy cottage, not spooky at all.

Albert lumbered over to the piano and sat down. Annah had to fight the impulse to look over at him. Mr. Sproul came back with glasses and a pitcher. No one spoke.

Finally Albert began to play. Annah didn't know what the music was, but it was lovely. It could have been Mozart, she thought; she wished she knew more about music. Whatever it was, she felt as if she could listen to it for hours. At first it was light, almost playful, full of what seemed to her like little musical jokes, musical versions of puns, and then it grew more serious, almost sad. Albert's touch was light and sure. He made no mistakes, as far as she could tell.

He stopped suddenly, as if in the middle of a sentence. He whirled around on the piano stool and said, "I'm thirsty. Can I have some Moxie?"

"It's all gone, Albie," his father said gently. "How about some of this nice cold sassy?"

"Albert," Annah said, "that was wonderful. Your music was wonderful."

He shrugged and laughed. "I played a concert down to Melrose last winter, didn't I, Dad? They gave me Boston cream pie afterwards. It was good, but not as good as my mother's."

"Was that Mozart you played just now?" Dodie asked.

"Naw. That was just something I made up."

Annah looked at Dodie, and she nodded.

"Albert makes up a lot of wonderful music."

When they had thanked the Sprouls and were ready to go, Albert suddenly said, "Look what I got!" He pointed to a pair of red mittens hanging from a hook. He put them on and waved his hands around. They were Annah's mittens. "What do you think of 'em?" Albert said. "Ain't they pretty? I found 'em."

Dodie looked at Annah.

"They're beautiful, Albie," Annah said. "They look nice on you."

"He wore them to bed the first week after he found them," his father said. "I couldn't get them off him."

"Next time you folks come up," Dodie said, "maybe I'll have my car fixed, and I'll take you for a ride."

Albert clapped his mittens together. "Good! We can go see The Old Man of the Mountain."

"Well," Dodie said a few minutes later, as Annah rowed toward home, "what'd you think?"

"I could hardly believe it. I almost thought it must be a player piano."

Dodie laughed. "No, it's the real McCoy. Sometimes people that can't see so well and kind of didn't grow up quite right, they have a lot of talent for music. I've read a lot about it."

When Annah told Aunt Edna about it, Aunt Edna nodded. "I've never heard Albert play, but Joe did, and he said it was remarkable. I'm glad you got to know Albert."

"To think I used to be so scared of him and that island," Annah said. "I used to have nightmares, even at home in the winter."

"I've got to go home," Dodie said, jumping up abruptly. "Thank you a lot for being so nice to me." And almost before Annah had time to say anything to her, she was gone, striding up the path and into the woods out of sight.

Aunt Edna watched her till she was gone. "I hope she'll be all right," she said.

Annah started to say that Dodie's cold seemed about gone, but it occurred to her that that was not what Aunt Edna meant.

CHAPTER 23

"YOUR friend's father is in the pokey again," Mabel Turner said, making a chant of it.

It was the Friday before the last week of school, and Dodie had not been around for a couple of days. Annah looked over her shoulder at Mabel. She was putting some books on the shelf in her locker, and turning made her drop one. Mabel laughed.

"Can't you ever say anything nice about people?" Annah asked. "What did Dodie ever do to you?"

"Moonshiners." Mabel sniffed. "Riffraff."

Annah lifted her hand angrily, but Homer grabbed her wrist. "Simmer down," he said quietly. "Don't let her rile you."

Mabel and her friends waltzed away, laughing loudly. Annah got a touch of satisfaction when she saw the traffic squad boy pull them out of line.

"Has he been arrested?" she asked Homer.

"I heard he had, yeah."

"I'd better go see if she's all right."

"If they put him away for long enough," Homer said, "I could do some work on that car of Dodie's."

"You like to work on cars?"

"Rather do it than eat. I went up there one day to look at it. Dodie asked me to. But the old man drove me off."

"I'll ask her if she wants you to now."

"Great. Thanks. All it needs is a few parts and some body work."

Annah picked up her bike at the filling station, where she parked it during the day. After the affair of the snowshoes, she was taking no chances on Mabel Turner or anyone else letting the air out of her tires or doing some other cute trick.

She stopped to get the mail. There was a short, excited letter from her mother, postmarked Palm Beach. She had gone to work for a month, on trial, just for expenses and commission, to see if she had any ability to sell real estate. "Mr. Bly says I'm a natural. I guess he means I've got the gift of gab. Well, we'll see. Wish me luck, sweetheart. I can see just a tiny glimmer of light at the end of the tunnel, at last."

Annah rode slowly, enjoying the day. Soon it would be warm enough to go swimming.

Yesterday the editor of the literary magazine had asked if she would be advertising manager next year. "It's not glamorous," the girl said, "but it's a foot in the door." She said Doris had recommended Annah.

Annah didn't know what to say. She didn't even know where she would be next year. But she thanked the editor and said, "If I'm still here, I'd love to."

"Are you thinking about going back to Massachusetts?"

"I don't know. Nothing is very settled right now." She hadn't talked to anyone but Dodie about her family's situation, but people in a small town seemed to know everything about everybody.

"I think we're going to offer Dodie a place on the editorial staff," the girl said. "That's supposed to be a secret." She grinned. "I'm lousy at keeping secrets."

"She deserves it," Annah said. She felt a twinge of envy, but she knew Dodie wrote better than she did.

She had told Tillie so. "I'm an okay, competent writer, I think, but Dodie has some kind of wild streak of genius." She had written that to Tillie because she wanted to be sure she owned up to it in her own mind, and putting it down on paper made it real.

She wondered what Dodie and her family would live on if that man stayed in jail long. There wouldn't be anything at all coming in.

She was thinking so hard, she didn't notice at first that there was another car parked in front of Dodie's house. A man and a woman were helping Dodie's mother into the back seat. The man put a couple of suitcases on the running board.

Dodie's mother saw Annah. She leaned out of the car and yelled, "Where's Dodie?"

Startled, Annah said, "I don't know. Isn't she here?"

"Come on now, everything's fine," the woman said to Dodie's mother, trying to urge her back on the seat.

"She kidnapped Tommy!" Dodie's mother shrieked.

"Let's go, John," the woman said. She climbed in beside Dodie's mother. The man got in, backed up the car to the road, and drove away.

Annah was confused. Who were they and where were they taking Dodie's mother? She went up to the house and knocked on the open door. There was no one inside. The house looked clean, but things were strewn around in confusion: children's clothes, cooking utensils, a shabby winter coat, a man's wool cap. It looked as if they had left in a hurry.

She called Dodie several times, but there was no sign of her or of the little boy. The only place she knew to look then was in the cave.

She walked her bike through the woods. It was quite different now, with wild flowers in bloom and new light green needles on the pines. It smelled so good, Annah couldn't stop taking deep breaths.

Maybe those people were friends, taking Dodie's mother for a ride. They didn't act too friendly though. They wouldn't arrest her too, would they?

When she got to the cave, no one was in sight. "Dodie? Hey, Dode, it's me. Are you in there?"

For a long minute there was no sound at all except the rapid chip-chip-chip of a chipmunk who sat on a stump watching her with bright eyes.

"Where's January?" she said to him.

He made a graceful leap to a hanging branch and scampered up the tree.

"Chip-chip . . ." It was a small, human voice.

Annah turned back quickly to the cave and saw a little boy in a flannel nightgown sitting in the entrance. He was about five years old, with a round face. His eyes were closed tight. Dodie's little brother. He was blind, and she had never said so.

"Move over and let me out, punkin." It was Dodie, coming out of the cave. Without any explanations she said, "What's happening at the house?"

"A man and a woman drove off with your mother."

"Did they ask if you'd seen me?"

"Your mother did."

"What'd you say?"

"No, of course. Dodie, what's going on?"

"It's the county."

"What do you mean?"

As she talked, Dodie kept her hand on the little boy, now and then glancing past Annah up the path.

"Well, they hauled the old man off to the clink again. He'll be there a long while this time. Resisting arrest. He put up one gosh-awful battle, I'll say that for him. And Ma went after 'em with a shotgun. They weren't too pleased." She gave a dry laugh.

"What will happen to your mother?"

For a moment Dodie rocked back and forth. "Assaulting the police with a deadly weapon . . . and she's done it before. But I think they'll put her in the county hospital. They know she's an alcoholic. Poor Ma, she's been so slammed around, she don't know which way is up." Her eyes filled with tears. "A person can only take so much." She dried her eyes on her sleeve. "They've been wanting to put Tommy away in the state hospital, but they aren't a-gonna do it, are they, Tombo?"

"Don't get Tommy," the child said.

"He's—" Annah hesitated. "He can't see, can he?"

"Blind as a bat. Born that way. But he's smart as a whip, aren't you, Tom?"

"But what will you do?"

"I'll tell you what I won't do. I won't let them bury Tom in some state hospital. I've seen those places. You might as well bury a person alive. God knows what would happen to him. But he's smart. Not what they call arrested, like Albie."

Annah wondered how she could tell. The child wasn't more than five, surely. But she didn't question Dodie.

"He might turn out to be a good musician like Albie. He can carry a tune already. Sing 'Farmer in the Dell,' Tom."

The thin childish voice sang the first bars on key.

"See?" Dodie said. "He might be some kind of genius."

"But what are you going to do now, the two of you?"

"First of all, swear on the Bible that you won't tell where we are."

"I haven't got a Bible here."

"You got one at home?"

"Sure."

"Then say, 'I, Annah Perry, swear on my Bible that's at home that I won't tell any soul whatsoever, not even Aunt Edna, where Dodie and Tommy are.' "

Annah repeated the words. "But what are you going to *do*?"

"Stay right here. Nobody but you knows about this cave. This time of year it's warm and cozy. I've been bringing stuff out here and stashing it away: Tommy's clothes, food, blankets, books. There's a spring right over there beyond where the chipmunk's sitting, and there's a stream a little farther on. We'll make out fine till I can think what to do."

"Dodie, you can't live like that."

"Who says I can't? If they knew where I have Tommy, they'd grab him. I'm not sixteen till next week, and anyway I think you have to be eighteen before they'll let you have any say-so."

Annah began to be excited about the adventure of it. If anyone could survive, Dodie could. And saving that pretty little boy from some cruel fate was a thing that had to be done.

"Listen," Dodie said, "I'd really like to get Homer to fix that car. With wheels under me, I could get so far away, nobody'd care where I was. I haven't done any crimes, after all."

"What should I tell him?"

"I've been thinking. Tell him I'm up in Canada, me and Tommy, staying with an aunt. Tell him I want to come back after a while and pick up the car." She leaned her cheek on Tommy's blond head, thinking. "Only thing is, I haven't got any money to pay him."

"I've got a little," Annah said.

"We don't use other folks' money," Dodie said sternly.

"You can pay me back."

"Well," Dodie said, "we'll draw up an IOU. I haven't got any paper here, so you write one, and I'll sign it."

"All right. Listen, I forgot to tell you, I think they're going to ask you to be on the lit magazine staff. They were asking where you were."

For a moment Dodie looked wistful. Then her expression changed. "Too late for that razzmatazz," she said.

"But where will you go?"

Dodie waved her hand airily. "Oh, we'll hit the road. I'm strong, I'm a good workhorse. I'll find something. Just remember, you don't know where I am. I got to hide out till the hoorah dies down."

"Don't worry, I won't tell."

Dodie looked down at Tommy's face. "He's cute, isn't he?" Her voice had softened.

"Yes, he is. He's a sweet little kid."

"He's all I got." Then Dodie's tone changed and she waved with her free hand as she led Tommy back into the cave. "Don't take any wooden nickels."

CHAPTER 24

"HOW'S DODIE?" Aunt Edna asked her that evening. "You haven't said anything about her."

"Oh, she's okay. She hasn't been in school for a couple of days, but she's all right."

Aunt Edna was looking at her. "I heard her stepfather got arrested, and they took her mother away."

Inwardly Annah groaned. She should have known; in a small town everybody knew everything. She wondered who had told her. Maybe Billy Fraser. It was his day to go around the lake in his boat, delivering groceries. Most of the cottages were occupied now, at least on weekends.

"What happened to the little brother?" Aunt Edna said.

"Well, some aunt of Dodie's came and got them." Annah looked away. It was not easy to lie to Aunt Edna. "She lives up in Canada some place. Dodie said she'd write."

"She got here pretty fast," Aunt Edna said. She pumped some water from the pump in the kitchen sink to wash away the soapsuds left from the dishwater.

"I guess she must live on the border." Annah put away the last of the dishes. "I've got to do my algebra. Boy, I hate algebra more every day."

As Annah was leaving the room, Aunt Edna said, "Annah, if Dodie's in any trouble, let me help, will you?"

"Trouble?" Annah tried to sound puzzled.

"She can't manage alone with that little boy. Billy Fraser says the child is blind."

"Dodie'll be all right." Annah longed to tell Aunt Edna the whole story. But she had a mental picture of her leather-bound New Testament with her name on the cover in gilt letters beside her bed at home. Only, of course, now it was in storage.

Upstairs, she lay on her bed trying to think. She would go through the woods to Dodie's cave. She'd better wear Herb's compass. It was easy to get turned around in the woods.

What could Dodie do? What would become of her? The more she thought about it, the more it worried her. Finally she sat up and wrote a long letter to Margaret, telling her all about Dodie except the part about the cave. It helped to write it all down. "I feel so stupid," she wrote, "because I can't think of how to help."

Well, tomorrow she would get word to Homer about the car. That would be a start. She would take some food to Dodie and Tommy. They probably didn't have much there. Maybe some milk and shredded wheat and apples, some candy or something good for Tommy. Poor little guy.

She woke early and asked Aunt Edna if she could take the rowboat to town.

Homer was at the gas station, where she usually left her bike. He was helping Sam Parish change a tire. She took him aside and gave him Dodie's message about the car. A grin spread across his face.

"Swell! I'll go out right away. Is anybody there?"

"No." She was glad he was not one to ask questions.

"I'll get right on it."

Annah went on up the street to the grocery store. It took her a while to make up her mind what she wanted, but the clerk was patient. Finally she settled for puffed rice, which would be light to carry, some cans of milk, dried apricots, animal crackers, and a big chocolate bar.

When she came out of the store, she ran into Mabel and her usual troop of followers. "Where you going?" Mabel said.

"Home." Annah tried to push past her.

Mabel fell into step beside her. "Where's Dodie?"

"How do I know?"

"Because you're her buddy. You better tell where she is. The authorities are looking for her."

"Well, you're not one of the authorities, so don't worry about it," Annah said. "Would you mind letting me by?" Mabel was crowding her toward the side of the road.

"Tell me where she is. I've been asked by the authorities to find her."

"Oh, sure," Annah said. But Mabel's questions made her uneasy. "Well, not that it's anybody's business, but she's gone to visit her aunt in Canada."

"In a pig's eye," Mabel said. "She doesn't have any aunt, in Canada or anywhere else."

"You know so much, why ask me?" Annah pushed past her and walked fast toward the dock. She was going in the wrong direction for the cave, but with Mabel on her trail, she had to pretend she was going home.

They followed her all the way to the dock. Sighing

with annoyance, she stowed the groceries under the bow seat and said, "Well, hello and good-bye."

Mabel sat down on an overturned dory. "It's such a nice day," she said sweetly to her friends. "Just let's sit here and watch Annah rowing her boat in the hot sun. And we can be thankful we live in the village." She laughed.

Annah bit her lip. There was no escape. She untied the boat, put one foot in, and pushed off. She felt like slamming one of the oars flat on the water so Mabel would get soaked, but she didn't. That would only let Mabel know she'd made her mad.

When she was halfway home, she could still see them sitting there, small black dots on the dock. There wouldn't be time to go back to Dodie's later, because she had promised to help Aunt Edna put up the big screens on the veranda. Once they were up and the hammock was hung, she could sleep in the hammock at night. She had always loved to do that. You could see the stars if you turned on your back, and you could hear the soft wash of the water against the shore, and all night the hammock swung gently like a cradle.

So she would have to wait till tomorrow to see Dodie. But what would she do with the groceries? Aunt Edna would be puzzled by puffed rice and animal crackers. Maybe she could say she had developed a sudden passion for them. Or, with any luck, she could hide them somewhere. After a moment, she thought of the ice compartment of the big ice chest.

The summer iceman had begun his deliveries, coming around in his big outboard, with cakes of ice under canvas. She always loved to watch him use the tongs to swing a big cake onto the leather apron across his shoulders and carry it to the house as if it were light as a feather. She would tuck the grocery bag behind the chunk of ice. He wouldn't be back again till next week.

She tried to be quiet as she pulled into the cove, docked the boat, and walked across the pine needles to the sun porch door. Billy Fraser's oldest boy had come by, taken off the winter shutters, and put up the screens on the sun porch, a sign that summer had really arrived.

She opened the heavy top of the ice chest and put the bag of groceries in, as far away from the chunk of ice as she could get it, so it wouldn't get soaked with melting ice. The bag made a slight bumping sound on the zinc-lined chest. Henry came to see what she was doing, but he didn't bark. So far, so good.

She turned toward the kitchen. Aunt Edna was standing there, her back to Annah, taking some iced tea glasses down from a high shelf. Annah couldn't tell whether she had seen what was happening on the porch or not.

"Hi," Annah said.

"Oh, hi, honey. Is it hot on the lake?"

"Kind of."

"I just made some iced tea. Help yourself."

About half an hour later when they were struggling with the big veranda screens, they heard an outboard put-putting toward their cove. Aunt Edna was holding the screen steady while Annah balanced on the railing and reached up to snap the metal fasteners in place.

"Oh, dear," Aunt Edna said, looking toward the

cove. "Who is it? I'm filthy." She had a streak of dirt across her forehead and her hair was rumpled.

"You look cute," Annah said, "and it's only Mrs. Turner and Mrs. Hunter."

"Oh, that's all right then." She giggled. "Cute, indeed!"

They finished the section of screen they were on, and then Annah ran down to the cove to help the visitors tie up their boat. Mrs. Hunter had brought mail, as she always did when she came down the lake.

"Land ho!" Mrs. Hunter called cheerfully as she scrambled out of the boat.

Mrs. Turner was always slower and more sedate. Anna gave her a hand up out of the boat. She had a hunch that this was not a casual visit.

A little later, over glasses of iced tea and Aunt Edna's molasses cookies, the real purpose came out.

"We're so concerned about Dodie and the little boy. Mabel says no one at school knows where she is. You and Dodie were such good friends, Annah dear, we thought you might know. We'd like to help."

Annah felt herself blush. She tried to sound matter-of-fact. "She mentioned an aunt in Canada. It all happened so fast. But I'm sure she's all right."

"Dodie seems like a very competent girl," Aunt Edna said.

"She's had to be, poor kid," Mrs. Hunter said.

"Well, we want to do all we can," Mrs. Turner said. "The county officials were inquiring of us, because they understood she was a friend of Mabel's."

With difficulty, Annah kept quiet.

"The little boy ought to be in an institution for

the blind," Mrs. Turner went on, placidly stirring her tea. "The Perkins Institute or some such place."

"Dodie loves him," Annah said.

"Of course she does. But she can't care for him alone. It's against the law, I think. Goodness knows how she'll manage for herself."

"Dodie's grandmother was a darling," Mrs. Hunter said. "And her real father was a fine man. But he fell for a pretty face and married Eugenia. Dodie's mother," she explained to Annah. "Eugenia was a good enough girl but weak, you know. And once she got in the clutches of that second husband . . ." She brushed the crumbs from her hands and stood up. "Well, Marge, we'd better be on our way." She pulled a couple of letters from her pocket. "One for Edna, one for Annah. And, oh yes, a postcard from your brother, reminding you that he'll be here on the fourth. Sounds as if he's enjoying life, that one." She shook her head. "I remember when he used to come into the post office and plague me by banging the letter slot. Drove me mad. But he sure was cute."

Her letter was from Margaret. She put it unopened in her pocket until she and Aunt Edna finished with the screens, and then she decided to go for a quick swim while the sun was up. The water was very cold, so she didn't stay in long, but it made her tingle and feel good.

Then, finally, she stretched out on the hammock and opened Margaret's letter. "Dear Annah: Did I tell you I'm on the night shift now that I'm head baker? I go on at four and get through at midnight. I like it. It makes me feel as if every day's a holiday. Get to bed around one, get up around eight, and nearly all day ahead of me. Miss Bartlett, the supervisor of the hospital, complimented me on my orange rolls. Next thing you know they'll be tapping me on the shoulder with a sword and calling me Dame Margaret. I'm thinking about taking a dietician course at the vocational school next fall. Now I got some more news. My sister Rosie's runaway hubby showed up with his hat in his hand and money in his pocket (best not to ask where he got it) and they are buying my house, a hundred down, fifty a month. What do you think of that? I got it in writing, and notarized, because I know Rosie's husband and I wasn't born yesterday. I can't live out of town and work the night shift. No trains. Also I decided, I'm sick of living here with all these women, ninety percent of whom snore so loud you'd think it was the freight train coming down the track. So next Monday I'm moving into a little rented house half a mile from the hospital. It's no palace but it beats my old shack. One parlor big enough to turn around in. One kitchen, biggest room in the house. One bedroom with a good view of the backside of Mullen's gas station. *And* one guest room, la-di-da, big enough so if you back into it and fall onto the bed, you'll fit. So any time you want to pay me a visit, I'm receiving. You'll get good orange rolls and some fried clams straight from Vin's place at Dane Street Beach. Yours truly, Margaret."

Annah lay still, thinking about Margaret's news. She seemed to be the only one of them that was doing better and better. It was great that she would have a little house of her own, near the hospital. Margaret always did like her privacy. She must have hated the

156

dorm. Maybe some day this summer she could take the train down to Beverly and spend a few days with her. Or . . . Annah suddenly sat up straight. The idea that had popped into her mind made her feel as if her hair were standing on end. If Margaret had an extra room, why couldn't she go and *live* with Margaret? Her father sent Aunt Edna money now and then; why couldn't he send it to Margaret instead? The high school in Beverly was near the hospital, and it was a big one. She'd be just five or six miles away from Tillie and Richie and everybody, twenty minutes by train or streetcar. She'd be in school while Margaret was home, so she wouldn't get in her hair. And she could clean house and cook and all that stuff so Margaret wouldn't have to bother. It sounded perfect!

She was so excited, she wanted to run in and tell Aunt Edna about it right away. But first she'd better see what Margaret had to say. Maybe she was planning to marry Johnny LeFaver after all, or somebody else, some handsome Irish orderly at the hospital, or maybe an intern. She had invited Annah to visit; she hadn't said anything about staying.

Well, with Margaret, the only way was to ask flat out. Annah went upstairs and got out her stationery. She'd make it short. "Dear Margaret: Wonderful news about your new house. You asked me to visit. How about asking me to live with you, starting next fall? I can pay and work my way. I won't be underfoot. I won't be sloppy or messy or untidy, and I'll cook and clean. I could go to BHS. Let me know PDQ. Or at least as soon as you have time to think it over. Love and SWAK, Annah."

If she rode her bike to town right now, she'd catch the evening mail train, and Margaret would get the letter in the morning. She made an excuse to Aunt Edna, who never questioned her anyway, and rode to town in record time, in spite of having to stop several times to say hello to some of the summer residents, who were beginning to move up.

It wasn't until she was nearly back to the cottage that she remembered she should have brought Dodie's food to her. She hadn't been thinking of anything except going home, living with Margaret, being with her old friends again. She felt ashamed of herself for being so forgetful of Dodie. First thing in the morning, she'd go to the cave, before anything could stop her.

CHAPTER 25

URING the night Annah woke to the sound of Henry whining and whimpering, and half an hour later there was a thunderstorm that seemed to shake the earth.

Aunt Edna lit the lamp and made a small fire in the stove to take the chill off. They wrapped themselves in quilts and ate fudge while the thunder crashed so close to the cottage, it seemed to be inside. Flashes of lightning lit up the whole end of the lake.

Alice curled up in front of the stove and went serenely to sleep, but Henry refused all invitations to come out from under Aunt Edna's bed.

"Joe always said we got it worse here on the point than anywhere on the lake," Aunt Edna said. "He always liked to go out on the veranda and watch the lake whip up. I'm not afraid of storms, at least not the way Henry is, but I'd just as soon stay inside while they're going on."

"Dad used to take us kids out on the porch," Annah said. "He was afraid we'd be scared of them, the way Mother is. You and Mother are so different, aren't you?"

"In many ways, I guess." Aunt Edna was silent for a minute. "Yesterday's letter sounded excited. I hope the real estate thing works out. Palm Beach has money, unlike most parts of the country. But real estate is iffy."

"She always says Dad is a good salesman, but she's the one who's really good. You ought to see her at the church bazaar. If there's anything that they're sure won't sell, the rector brings it to Mother. He knows she'll sell it to somebody."

When the storm died away, the last crashes growing fainter as it moved farther inland, they went back to bed. The rain didn't stop. Annah lay awake listening to it thundering on the roof like fists. At least Dodie would be dry in the cave. She wondered if Tommy was afraid of the storm.

In the morning, the rain was still coming down in a torrent so heavy it looked like a silver sheet.

"No going anywhere today," Aunt Edna said, as Henry dashed back into the house, dripping water, his tail between his legs. "My poor Henry, dear old Hank, you ought to live in the desert, where you could chase roadrunners and never get sprinkled on."

"Did you ever live in the desert?" Annah asked her. Her mind wasn't really on the conversation. She was thinking of Dodie. The rain had brought much cooler weather. And she and Tommy would be penned up in that cave, unable to get out and walk around.

"Once, one winter in California, near a little place called Indio, Joe got some wonderful pictures. I wrote some copy, and we sold the package to *Life*. It was great fun. Date palms; I'll never forget those marvelous juicy dates."

Annah wanted to say something to match the happy look of remembering on Aunt Edna's face, but she couldn't think of anything good enough. If you said, "Well, you were lucky to have all that happiness while you had it," that wasn't very comforting when you didn't have it anymore.

After breakfast they decided to use the rainy day to spring clean. They washed every dish, every pot and pan, every glass in the cottage, and then scrubbed the softwood floors and the kitchen linoleum, dusted all the corners, took down the pictures and dusted the tops.

By late afternoon they were tired and hungry. Aunt Edna boiled some potatoes, opened a can of corn, fried some onions and bits of salt pork, and produced a delicious corn chowder for an early supper. Annah kept thinking of Margaret.

In the middle of the meal Aunt Edna said, "You're worrying about Dodie, aren't you."

Annah was surprised. Dodie hadn't been mentioned all day. But she *had* been worrying. The rain showed no sign of letting up. "Oh, I expect she's having a good time at her aunt's in Canada," Annah said.

"Yes." Aunt Edna was giving all her attention to buttering a piece of bread. "Quite a few people in town are truly concerned about Dodie. They like her. They're hunting for her to help, not to harm her in any way."

Annah got up and refilled her chowder bowl. She didn't like to be cagey with Aunt Edna. But she had sworn on the Bible. She had given her word. "I suppose they would take Tommy away from her," she said. "If she were here, I mean."

"Yes, I suppose they would, but it would be best for both of them, I should think. There are some excellent schools for little chaps like Tommy. The one Albert Sproul goes to, or at least went to—he may have graduated by now—did wonders for him."

"Dodie loves Tommy," Annah said. "He's all she's got."

Aunt Edna didn't answer for a moment. "At one time or another, I suppose we all feel we've lost all we've got, but there's more, you know. What's gone is never replaced, but life holds a great many things, some of them quite unexpected." She gave Annah a sudden smile. "Who would have dreamed, for instance, that I would have the joy of your being here this year?"

Annah was taken aback. "You mean it hasn't been a bother?"

"Oh, Annah. You'll never know what a lifesaver you've been. Despair is insidious, especially when you're alone. It sneaks into your bones like a cold wind."

Annah was touched. "I didn't know you felt like that." But she was also troubled. What would happen if she moved to Beverly? She hadn't even thought about that. "What would you do if I weren't here? Like if Daddy whisked us all home again with a magic wand? Would you feel in despair again?"

"No, I'm over the hump, I think. I'll probably find other things to feel sorry for myself about from time to time, but this attack is on its way to convalescence."

Dodie! Annah thought. Aunt Ed and Dodie liked each other. Maybe Dodie could stay with her if she still needed somebody. That would solve two problems at once. Except for Tommy. And except that she'd better hold her horses till she heard from Margaret.

"When you leave," Aunt Edna said, as if she had been reading Annah's mind, "I'll probably push on too. One of these days it'll be time to get this show on the road again, as Joe would say." She scratched Henry, who was curled up in her lap. "Henry and I are gypsies."

"What about Alice?"

"Alice is a parochial cat. She won't leave town. Charlotte Hunter has first dibs on Alice."

So that was that. For a minute there Annah thought she had everybody fixed up, everybody, at least, except little Tommy.

In the morning it was still pouring. Rain thundered on the roof, and the waves rolled in and smashed against the shore almost like the beach at Dane Street after a storm. The road to town was impassable, and there was no question of taking out the boat. Aunt Edna and Annah played double solitaire and made fudge and discussed the articles Herb had been sending them about the coming presidential election. Herb was sure that Governor Roosevelt was going to solve the problems of the country.

At last the weather cleared. It was the next to last day of school. Annah found that the food she had bought for Dodie had gotten soaked in the melting ice. Only the apricots and possibly the very damp chocolate bar seemed worth salvaging. She packed them in her pockets.

Because so many people hadn't been able to get to school during the rain, all kinds of things were crammed into those last two days, from final exams to announcements by the student council and the magazine to prolonged farewells to the seniors who were going away to college. Annah got through the first day as fast as she could, and then ran all the way to the grocery store, praying that she wouldn't meet Mabel again.

Before she got to the store, she ran into police chief LeBlanc and Billy Fraser, sitting on the town hall steps having a smoke. They both called out to her, and the chief stopped her.

"You're just the one I'm looking for," he said.

"Me?" Annah wondered if she had broken some law.

"Yeah. Sit down a minute."

She hesitated. "Is this official? I'm in an awful hurry. . . ."

"It's official." But he smiled and patted the granite steps beside him.

She sat down, feeling anxious.

"It's about your friend Dodie."

"Oh." She looked at him sideways. Had he found her? Had they taken her away after all?

"Seems like the County folks were looking for her, mainly on account of the little fella. Their mother will be in the alcoholic ward for quite a spell. He needs taking care of. Anyway, nobody knew where Dodie'd gone. But Mabel Turner decided to find out . . ." He grinned when Annah groaned. "She seen it as her civic duty, you might say."

"You might say," Annah said grimly.

"Well, she's got proof, she says, that they're hiding out somewheres near the house."

"But she doesn't know where?" Annah began to smile.

"No, but knowing Mabel, it ain't going to take her long. I figured you might know, and if you do, it might be a favor to Dodie to let me in on it. I'm pretty good at holding off those County folks, and I just dropped in on your aunt Edna to see if she'd put up those two kids for a little bit, till we get things straightened out. Said she would. I guess she suspects you know where Dodie is. Now if you can talk Dodie into coming out into the open, we'll be all set."

164

"Have to do something about that car," Billy Fraser said.

"It's really Dodie's car," Annah said. "Her grandmother gave her the registration."

"Well, will you haul her out of wherever she is?" Billy stood up. "I'll drive you up to the house. I s'pose she's someplace close by?"

"I can't tell you where."

"I know that. Let's go."

Annah felt relieved. She could keep her promise and still take care of Dodie and Tommy. She climbed into Billy's car.

CHAPTER 26

CHIEF LEBLANC and Billy stayed in the car in Dodie's yard while Annah went to talk to her. They had come in Billy's old car instead of the police car, so as not to alarm Dodie.

As she walked down the path to the cave, Annah's optimism began to fail. It had sounded so safe and so sensible, but it was really only temporary. What would happen to Dodie and Tommy after their "few days" at Aunt Edna's?

If Homer could get the car ready within that time, maybe they could think of something. Perhaps if Dodie went to New York, Herb could help her. He was spending his time finding living quarters for refugees, and Dodie was a kind of refugee, wasn't she? Maybe she could write him and ask him.

But first she had to reassure Dodie. She hadn't really broken her promise. She hadn't told the chief about the cave.

When she came to it, there was no sign of Dodie. The woods were still dripping from the days of rain, and the ground was soggy. There was a lot of water at the mouth of the cave. Maybe they had been flooded out. But where had they gone? She felt guilty that she hadn't found some way to come to Dodie's rescue before this. What if they had run out of food?

She called and called, but there was no answer. Not even January was visible. But suddenly a chipmunk dashed past her and chattered up a tree, peering at her with bright eyes.

Then she saw January, just his twitching ears visible behind a bush.

"January, where'd they go?" And again she called, "Dodie!"

"Looking for somebody?"

She whirled around. Dodie was right behind her, looking dirty and dishevelled, but grinning. "Dodie! I thought you'd gone."

"We hid. I heard a motorcar."

"Where's Tommy?"

Dodie pointed to a rock where Tommy lay on a blanket, fast asleep. "It's like a duck blind, only a Tomblind. Bushes to hide him. Where have you been? We're starved. And all our clothes are wet. Did you bring food?"

"Listen, Dodie . . ." She didn't know how to begin. "That car you heard . . ." She saw the look of alarm on Dodie's face. Then Dodie looked past her and froze.

"Hi, Dodie." It was Chief LeBlanc. He spoke gently. "Don't panic now. . . ."

But Dodie had already begun to run. She had to go to the rock first to grab Tommy. The chief got there ahead of her. He seized her arm.

Dodie turned her head and looked at Annah. "You traitor," she said in a deadly quiet voice.

"No, she ain't. You just simmer down now and listen," the chief said. "She didn't tell me where you were hid out. I followed her. We got a solution for you and the little guy."

"Sure." Dodie looked crumpled, as if she could hardly stand up.

Billy Fraser came up behind them. "Hi, Dodie. Harry, these kids need something to eat. We can talk later. Come on, Dodie, you know you can trust me."

"I trust nobody," Dodie said, her voice low.

Billy picked up the sleeping child. "Let's go."

"Dodie," Annah said, "you don't understand. They're on your side."

"Cops?" Dodie's lip curled.

"The chief fixed it so you and Tommy can stay with Aunt Edna awhile, till things get straightened out."

"What about the County?"

"All taken care of. Come on, now, Dodie. I'm gettin' hungry myself just standing here." The chief led her gently toward the path.

By the time Dodie had had a steak sandwich, French fries, and a chocolate malted, and Tommy had had soup and a toasted cheese sandwich, she was in more of a mood to listen.

Chief LeBlanc explained to her that he had talked to the County people and had taken responsibility for Tommy and her for the time being.

"What comes after 'the time being'?" Dodie asked.

"Worry about that later," Billy Fraser said. "There's a lot of folks willing to help. Let 'em."

"Help how?"

Billy told her that Mrs. Hunter and some of the other ladies in the church were planning a rummage sale to raise a little money for her.

"We don't take charity," Dodie said.

"Oh, Dode, get down off your high horse," the chief said. "These days, we all help each other best as we can. It's like a barn-burning, only this time it's our savings that got eaten up. So we tide each other over. You're no better than the rest of us, so don't go slapping down a helping hand."

Dodie blinked. "All right," she said meekly. "But I'll pay it back when I can."

"That's the ticket. Finish off that pie and let's go."

They went to Aunt Edna's cottage in style, in the chief's new outboard, towing Annah's boat. "My old boat," he told them above the racket of the motor, "got stove up and sank in the cove, and the engine gave out, all in the same week."

For the first time since they had picked her up, Dodie smiled.

Annah leaned back in the stern, trailing her fingers in the water. It had been a long time since she felt really relaxed. Other people were concerned about Dodie; somebody would come up with some idea that would take care of them. And she had Margaret's new house to think about. If she rode her bike the back way, up Brimbal Avenue, she could get to Til's house in maybe an hour. She took a deep breath, and it seemed almost as if she could smell the salt wind off the beach. She'd stuff herself all summer on salt water taffy and ice cream cones and hot dogs, and swim every day and lie on her stomach on the sand and get a gorgeous tan.

In all the excitement of getting Dodie, she hadn't had a chance to go to the post office. She wondered if there were a letter from Margaret.

CHAPTER 27

DODIE had a cold, and Tommy had the croup. They were in bed upstairs, and Annah had moved into the downstairs bedroom.

Mr. and Mrs. Turner came over to see if they could help, and Chief LeBlanc sent the doctor to look at Tommy. The house smelled of steam and benzoin.

Annah skipped the last day of school. Nothing was going to happen anyway. So it was two days before she went to the post office. Then she had errands to do for Aunt Edna, so she didn't feel guilty about leaving, but she was very glad to get away. Her mother always said, "Annah will never be a nurse. She's too finicky and too impatient." And she was right.

She took the canoe, which was faster and a lot more fun than the heavy old rowboat.

And she grew more and more excited as she got nearer town, thinking about the letter she would surely have from Margaret. It had been days since she had sent her own, and the mail usually arrived the next day. Of course, there could be lots of reasons why Margaret might not like having Annah live with her. But no matter how hard she tried to brace herself against a negative answer, Annah's hopes were high.

There was a lot of mail, for her and for Aunt Edna, but Annah couldn't look at it right away because Mrs. Hunter was feeling talkative, and then Mrs. Turner joined them, wanting to know if Dodie and Tommy were any better.

"We're having the rummage sale tomorrow," Mrs. Hunter said. "We've got a lot of stuff. Plenty of it's junk, but you'd be surprised how folks value junk as long as it's not their own."

"Still and all," Mrs. Turner said, "it's only a drop in the bucket. We haven't got Dodie's problems solved by a long shot. Something will have to be done about Tommy."

Annah sneaked a quick look at the letters in her hand, and saw Margaret's careful handwriting. In fact, it looked as if there were two letters from Margaret. She was tingling with impatience.

"If she could only get a job waitressing in one of the resort hotels," Mrs. Turner went on. "We talked to a friend of ours who's a chef at the Jackson Falls House, but he says business is off something wicked."

"Nobody's got any money," Mrs. Hunter said.

"A nice place as a maid would be good for Dodie . . ."

Shocked, Annah interrupted. "Maid! But Dodie's smart."

"I know, honey, but we have to face facts. Plenty of smart people are digging ditches these days."

The picture of Dodie in some menial job, Tommy in a state institution where nobody cared about him, suddenly struck Annah with such force she had to excuse herself and get out of there.

Homer was just coming down the street. "Listen," he said, "tell Dodie the auto's coming along good. Chief LeBlanc let me tow it down to the station, where I could work on it right. I got the mudguard about shaped up. I been having trouble with the timer, but I think she ought to percolate in a couple days now."

Annah was having trouble keeping her mind on what he was saying. She wanted to read her mail. "Good. I'll tell her, Homer. She'll be real glad."

"And tell her it won't cost her a dime. I haven't had so much fun in my life." He went down the street, whistling.

Annah decided to read her letters back at the dock, so she wouldn't be interrupted. After buying the things at the drugstore that Aunt Edna wanted, she almost ran to the dock.

She sat on the edge, her legs hanging over, the toes of her sneakers touching the water. She looked at the postmarks on Margaret's two letters, and opened the earlier one first. It was short.

"Dear Annah: Got your letter today. Busy moving so haven't got much time to write, but you know you are welcome and then some, to stay with me one day, fifty days, or all the days of your life. You didn't need to ask. Do you still like warmed-up maple syrup on your waffles? Yrs, Margaret."

Annah almost yelled for joy. She kicked the water up into a spray with her toes. It was true! She could go live with Margaret . . . be with her old friends . . . go to a good school like BHS! It was almost too good to believe.

"What are you sitting on the dock for?"

She jumped to her feet. It was Mabel, alone. Why did it always have to be Mabel? "Do you follow me around or what?" she said, but even Mabel couldn't really upset her at this moment.

"How long do you guys have to put up with those kids?" Mabel said. "Not long, I guess. The County's got plans for 'em, I heard. Well, we don't need riffraff in this town."

Annah decided to ignore her. She moved a little away, closer to where her canoe was pulled up on the beach, and sat on a rock. She opened Margaret's second letter. "Excuse me," she said pointedly, "I have some important mail to read."

"Sure, sure." Mabel's tone was sarcastic. "Everything about you is always so important. Just because your father was a banker. Well, now he's unemployed like any ordinary bum, ha ha."

Annah wasn't listening. She had started to read Margaret's second letter. "Dear Annah: I got your two letters wrong way around. That big bimbo, the postman, keeps forgetting I've moved. Anyways about your friend Dodie. I felt real bad the way you described her and the little blind feller. I know how it feels not to know which way to turn. What I was thinking, and now you're the one has to decide this, and whatever you say is all right with me. You know how much I want you to come stay with me, but you do have a good home there with Mrs. Edna, and Dodie's got nothing. If she wanted me to put her up for a little while, I couldn't undertake to do it forever but just till she gets settled, why, she could stay here. I could probably get her a little work washing dishes at the hospital, seeing I've got an inside track there now, ha ha, and she could look around. You remember the school for the blind here. Well, I went in bold as brass and talked to our supervisor and she called the school. They don't usually take 'em that young, but she pulled rank and talked 'em into it. The cost is very small, and they waive it in some cases. It's

173

mostly privately endowed. Richie's dad is on the board, which won't hurt any. When the little guy is big enough, he'll learn Braille and how to cane chairs so he can earn a living. They need the child's mother to sign a paper if possible, but I guess that could be done. The catch to all this is, I don't have room for two people. And you have to decide this one, my Annie-banany. I know how much you want to come back. You know, though, it wouldn't be the same. My house is about as big as your old kitchen. You'd have the high school here to get used to. The hours I work, you'd be alone a lot. Well, that's it. Let me know what you decide, and the decision is just between you and me—a secret, like we always had. Love, Margaret."

When she looked up, Mabel was still there.

"Who's it from that's so important?" Mabel peered at the envelope in Annah's lap. "It doesn't look like very educated handwriting. You know some peculiar people, Annah."

Annah stood up and gave Mabel a hard shove. Taken by surprise, Mabel lost her balance, staggered backward, and fell into the cove with a great splash. Annah got into the canoe and paddled furiously toward the cottage.

CHAPTER 28

AT FIRST it had not been easy to talk Dodie into staying with Margaret and putting Tommy in the school. She kept saying she wouldn't be separated from Tommy.

"Not even two miles?" Annah was getting sick of arguing with her to do something that she wished with all her heart Dodie wouldn't do. But she had thought and thought about it, and there didn't seem to be any alternative. Apparently Margaret didn't expect Dodie to stay long, so, as Annah kept telling herself, maybe she could move to Margaret's after Dodie left.

"How often could I see him?" Dodie said.

"How do I know?"

"How do I know I'd get along with this Margaret? I don't take to rich folks."

Finally it was Aunt Edna who lost patience. "Dodie, Margaret is far from rich. She's a working girl with a big heart. She's trying to help you out, till you can get on your feet. And Tommy will be properly taken care of. Besides, it's just as stupid and snobbish to say you don't like people because they're rich—whatever that means these days—as it would be to say you don't like them because they're poor."

Dodie looked startled at Aunt Edna's tone, but she stopped complaining. "All right. I'll go. As soon as Tommy's better." A minute later she looked self-consciously at Annah and said, "Thanks for going to all the trouble."

A week later, when Tommy was well and the car was ready, Aunt Edna and Annah took Dodie and Tommy to town to start their journey. It had been agreed that Homer would go with her to Beverly, to help drive and in case something went wrong with the car. He would come back on the train. Mr. Turner had offered to pay his fare, but Homer's father worked for the railroad and had a family pass.

A couple of dozen people had gathered to see Dodie off. Her spirits soared when she saw them.

"Look, Tom! It's a send-off!"

Tommy looked around with his eyes shut tight, smiling happily. If Dodie liked it, he liked it.

The car had been properly registered, and after two attempts in Wolfeboro, Dodie had passed her driver's test, although Homer told Annah, "The inspector's hair turned white before we got through."

A new suitcase on the running board was a farewell present from the Turners, and Aunt Edna had bought some clothes to fill it. The money from the raffle was in a check that Billy Fraser had told her a dozen times to be sure to take straight to the bank and use to open a checking account.

Mrs. Hunter closed the post office for the occasion, and Eloise, the "central" at the telephone exchange, closed up for half an hour.

"All we need is a brass band," Dodie said, but she was beaming with pleasure and full of activity. She changed the position of the suitcase several times, until it finally fell off the running board, and Homer patiently put it back where it had been in the first place.

Some of the students from school showed up, among

them Jamie and Doris. In the background, Annah saw Mabel, alone and apart from the others.

Dodie got in behind the wheel and tucked Tommy in beside her, leaving room for Homer on the passenger side. "Let's get this caravan moving!" Dodie shouted.

Homer got the crank and went to the front of the car. He twirled it, but nothing happened.

Somebody yelled, "Set the spark."

Dodie fiddled with the various levers. Homer came and adjusted something. Once again he cranked, and this time the engine roared and rattled into life. The car began to move. Dodie yelled. People fled out of the way. Homer jumped into the seat, over the closed door, waved, and they were on their way. The crowd shouted their good-byes. Dodie turned to wave to them and headed straight for the ditch.

Chief LeBlanc screamed an anguished, *"Homer!"* almost in Annah's ear.

But Homer already had his hand on the wheel. The car jerked back onto the road.

Annah heard Billy Fraser mutter, "Dear Lord, get them there in one piece."

Aunt Edna was laughing. "Stop worrying. Homer is the most competent boy in New Hampshire."

"I just hope this lady she's going to stay with has got a steady disposition," Chief LeBlanc said. He took off his police cap and mopped his forehead.

"She has," Annah said.

"Dodie's all right," Aunt Edna said. "She's just excited today. She's just had her life saved, after all, and Tommy's too."

"Well, bless their hearts," Mrs. Hunter said. "Back to work."

After everyone scattered, Aunt Edna and Annah stopped at the drugstore to have a soda and cool down. They looked at each other.

"Seems quiet, doesn't it," Annah said.

"It does indeed." A moment later, Aunt Edna looked down at her soda, making a business of trying to spear the cherry with her straw. Without looking at Annah, she said in a low voice, "I have a good idea of what you gave up for Dodie and Tom. I just want to say that I like you about as much as anybody I've ever known." Then she called to the druggist: "Mr. Q., how much do we owe you for this sumptuous repast? And while I'm about it, I need some of that good stuff for sunburn."

Neither she nor Annah ever again referred to the circumstances behind Dodie's departure.

CHAPTER 29

ERB came for the Fourth of July weekend, hitchhiking all the way from New York with only three changes, as he told them proudly. He looked much the same, though perhaps a little thinner and somehow older. He came wearing his familiar tweed jacket, white shirt, flannel pants.

"Till they wear out," he said, when Annah commented.

"Who launders your shirts?"

"Who do you think? Yours truly. You think laundry is some mystical process only women can fathom?" He kissed Aunt Edna's cheek and said, "I'm going swimming. I've been dreaming of it for days."

He came back a little later, shivering. "I forgot how cold it is! But good!" Minutes later he was on the veranda with them, in clean khaki pants and a blue shirt that matched his eyes. Annah had forgotten, she thought, how handsome he was.

"All right, friends," he said, stretching out full length on the deck chair on the dock. "You want news. I got news."

"What news?" Annah said.

He held up his hand. "Patience. I am about to tell it. First, I stopped in Beverly. Margaret is flourishing. She's fatter, she's feistier, she's an even better cook, if possible, and her house is clean, functional, and comfortable."

"And Dodie . . . ?" Annah had had only one short letter from Dodie, and Margaret's letters had given her only the details of their arrival.

"Dodie seems to be fine. She's a quiet kid, isn't she."

Annah and Aunt Edna exchanged glances. "Only sometimes," Annah said.

"Well, maybe I awed her. I'm pretty awesome, we all agree. Seriously, she seems relaxed. She's tanned, she looks well, and seems to feel at home with Margaret. They divvy up the work around the place and all seems serene. The little boy had some adjustment problems, but apparently he's doing better. In short, it seems to be working." He looked at Annah. "Margaret said some nice things about you, but I won't embarrass you by repeating them."

Before Annah could beg him to tell her what Margaret had said, he went on. "But that's the little news. The big news—good or bad, depending on your point of view—our house has been sold."

"Sold!" Annah stared at him. It had gone unsold for such a long time, she had unconsciously begun to think it never would happen. Yet she wasn't engulfed in a wave of grief, as she would have expected. Instead, she felt detached, almost floating, like a balloon that's broken away from the person holding the string. She tried to imagine other people living in the house, in her room, seeing her initials carved on the windowsill. Some people didn't like round rooms. She couldn't decide whether it was worse to think of people living there or think of it empty.

"Did your father get a decent price?" Aunt Edna asked.

"Considering the times. He cleared around eight grand, after the commission."

"It sounds like a lot of money," Annah said.

Herb smiled. "It's been awhile since even eight *hundred* seemed real. Or eighty. Or eight."

"What does that do to their plans?" Aunt Edna asked the question that Annah was about to ask.

"I think Dad would like to hide it under the mattress." Herb laughed. "But our mother has plans a-plenty. She fancies herself a hotshot real estate saleswoman now, although so far she hasn't sold anything. She's full of stories of how so-and-so, 'the well-known millionaire,' *almost* bought some property from her. Anyway, she's persuaded Dad to venture part of the house money. He's going to join her in Palm Beach, and they're going to go into business. She'll sell, he'll be the business manager, do the bookkeeping, all that arcane stuff that he's so good at."

In a small voice Annah said, "What about me?"

"Well, I'm instructed to tell you that if you want to gamble on the high life in Palm Beach, you can go down as soon as they find an apartment. They want you to understand that they miss you and want you. However, Dad, who is not as optimistic as Mother, cautions that it might be hard. Probably a small apartment, who knows how much available money, who knows what kind of school, etcetera etcetera. In short, for you, it's a pig in a poke, as they say."

"Annah," Aunt Edna said, "you are welcome here as long as you want to stay, you know that."

"In any case," Herb said, "wait awhile. The whole thing could blow up in two months. If it doesn't look as if it'll pay off, Dad won't pour much money down the drain, I'm sure of that."

Annah tried to think about living in Florida, but all she got was a blur.

Herb finished the iced coffee Aunt Edna had given him. "Aunt Ed, are you going to settle down here forever?"

"Oh, no. It was a kind of hiatus, I guess. One of these days I'll move. Maybe to Havana for a while. Joe and I talked about going to Cuba. He knew Hemingway, and Hemingway was so keen on Cuba." She looked at Annah. "Maybe you'd like to go with me. It's only ninety miles from Florida." She got up. "But nobody has to make any decisions now, thank goodness." She checked the fireworks. "Everything's here, I guess."

Annah lay back in the deck chair and thought about how odd it was to have options about her future. Such a short time ago it had seemed so settled: She would go on to Wellesley; Richie would go to Harvard; Peter would go to MIT; Til would be at Radcliffe or Smith. They would go to football games in Cambridge, and tea-dances at the Copley Plaza, and the Harvard Jubilee, where you danced all night and had breakfast by the ocean as the sun came up. . . . It didn't seem real anymore. It sounded attractive, just as it always had, but not real. She tried to think of Dodie being interested in any of that, and she almost laughed aloud. She tried to think of Homer in a dinner jacket at a formal dance. It wasn't that he couldn't bring it off if he tried; it was just that she was pretty sure he'd find it boring. He'd rather be fixing a car. Even Richie had written her the other day that he had made his mother mad by quitting dancing school. "It made me feel like some pal of Marie Antoinette in the French Revolution. It's kid stuff. Fantasy."

She heard Herb strike a match, and smelled the sharp sulphur smell, then the smell of his pipe tobacco. She wanted to go to college, she knew that, maybe still Wellesley, but for different reasons. She wasn't all that great a writer, she knew that now. Maybe she could be a reporter. She wanted to see the world Herb talked so much about. She wanted to understand why good people had to run away from their own countries and come here to keep from getting killed. There was a lot she wanted to know, and really, she didn't know anything at all.

She felt sleepy suddenly. But they had to wait for midnight. It was the night before the Fourth, and it was traditional for all the cottagers to set off their fireworks over the lake at midnight, right after Colonel Darcy set off his little cannon.

After a while, she heard Herb say quietly, "It's been hard on Annah, all the changes."

She realized they thought she was asleep.

"She's done fine," Aunt Edna said. "She's grown up a lot. She wanted desperately to go live with Margaret—she didn't say so, but I know she did. She gave it up for Dodie and the little boy."

"Maybe it's for the best," Herb said. "Growing up comfortable can be a handicap."

Aunt Edna laughed. "I'm too old to scorn comfort."

"Yes, but you know the score. I hope she sticks with you."

BAM! The roar of Colonel Darcy's cannon echoed across the lake.

"Here we go!" Herb ran to set off the rockets that Aunt Edna had bought.

All around the lake the sky lit up with soaring flares of light and color as the cottagers responded to their cue. Shooting stars and constellations shot into the sky and unfolded, twisting, arcing, hissing, and dying out as new bursts replaced them.

The show went on for about a half hour. It lifted Annah's spirits. It made the world seem bright and new and full of surprises.

Finally the display faded, falling dazzles of light ending with a small hiss as they hit the water. Then there was a pause for the final display that would come from the colonel's dock.

The lake was silent and dark. Then far down the lake a loon's eerie laughter added a different note to the night. Annah felt the suspense. The only lights now were the lanterns on the docks around the shore, and one on the island burning brightly.

"Thar she blows!" Herb said.

From the colonel's dock, rockets flared into the sky and spread into a huge, fantastic dragon. Annah could almost hear the "ahs!" around the lake, as everyone looked up at the sky.

Then as the fierce, brightly colored dragon blurred and faded, another burst produced a big American flag. The show was over.

"I'm going to make scrambled eggs," Aunt Edna said. She headed for the cottage.

Annah felt too stirred to move. The world was so full of things. She had forgotten all about that wonderful night-before-the-Fourth celebration up here. "Why is it so terrific?" she said.

184

Herb shrugged. "We're all kids. We love to say 'ooh!'"

But that wasn't it. It was something bigger, but she didn't know what, and she was too hungry to sit there and think about it.

"Don't worry about the family," Herb said. "The whole country is in for a big change. Wait till Roosevelt gets in, you'll see. I smell coffee." He ran lightly up the path to the cottage.

When Herb talked, he always seemed to see the whole globe. You could almost hear the metallic sound as history shifted gears.

She put up the collar of her cotton sweater. It was nice the way the nights got cool here, even after the hottest days.

Along the shore, the lanterns were going out. People were going back into their cottages for scrambled eggs or a cup of coffee or to fight or make love or just talk about the fireworks. "Were they better than last year or not? Remember the ones two years ago?" Did they think about what they would be doing a year from now, or a month? Did the planet tilt under their feet?

She looked over at the island. The lantern on the Sprouls' dock was still lit. She thought about Albie. He would miss Dodie. She'd go see him, take him a bottle of Moxie, and ask him to play for her.

As she watched, she could just barely make out a figure on the Sprouls' dock. From the size of it, it was Albert. She saw the faint glint of a sparkler. It waved in the air for a moment and then sputtered. She saw it flung out over the lake as it died. She smiled. "Never mind, Albie. Better luck next year."